The Raven of Revenge

David Beaumont

Copyright © 2019 David Beaumont

All rights reserved.

ISBN:9871704723150

March 1603.

As the days of winter were slowly ending, so too the days and years of Queen Elizabeth were coming to a close. Feeling depressed and unwell she had retired to her favourite palace at Richmond where she refused to take to her bed but instead, willful to the last, was eased down onto cushions that lay scattered on the floor.
After four days she became too weak to resist when her ladies in waiting gently lifted her to her bed. Once there, still not speaking, she turned her face to the wall.
On the 24th day of March as a new spring started to come to the realm that she had ruled for forty five years, she died, and with her the dynasty and age of the Tudors.
The fears that for so long had surrounded the succession proved groundless as James Vl of Scotland, the thirty seven year old son of Mary Queen of Scots, the long since executed rival and claimant to Elizabeth's throne was proclaimed King James 1st of England.
As the early weeks of April passed, the retinue of the Royal procession progressed slowly stage by stage down through the country that James was now to rule. He was full of interest and wonder as they journeyed down through the land that after so many years of uncertainty he had finally, almost effortlessly inherited. As they made their way towards London and his coronation in Westminster Abbey he spoke endlessly to his courtiers of the many changes he would bring about in his new

Kingdom.

He was a strange mixture. A man of intellect and learning with a questioning mind, and yet of one thing he had not a doubt, and that was that he was divinely chosen for this role and that once duly anointed he would be answerable to none other than the God who had against so many odds, brought him to this time and place. In return, he would do God's work here in his new kingdom, and part of that work would be to cleanse and rid the land of God's enemies.

Among the most precious possessions held within the oak trunks of his baggage train were copies of "Daemonology" the book that he had himself written in which he described all the evils that stemmed from witchcraft and its practitioners.

For these there would be no mercy nor hiding place. He would have them sought out. He would have them found and punished. He would have then destroyed.

He was God's representative on earth.

Part 1 Prologue.

February 1609.

Martha knew she was running from death.
Every time she stumbled and fell. Every time there seemed to be no more breath in her. When the aching in her body screamed out at her to stop and to try and find a temporary shelter from the now endlessly driving snow and rest for just a few moments to tend the baby she clutched beneath her cloak, she knew it was impossible. She was running from death.
...and death always wins.

It had been a blustery mid February late afternoon with just a few scattered flakes of light snow already starting to fall when she had left, hoping that she would be able to get far away from the village before she was missed, but the night had closed in, the weather had worsened and as the snow had become heavier and begun to settle, roads that she thought she had known so well all her life, suddenly seemed changed, different and strange. She knew that if, or rather when she was pursued, then the road that led towards Honiton would probably be the first direction they would look for her and so she had taken the smaller lane that led from the village and went over the surrounding hills and on towards Exeter by a more southerly route. She had kept to the track for the first few hours in the hope that a carter would pass and show kindness to her and the baby, letting them ride at least some of the way towards Exeter where she had told herself she might find some place of safety, but the track remained empty.

Though she had never been there and only heard it spoken of, the ancient city of Exeter with its great Cathedral, its castle, and grand houses, offered the promise of all she needed. There would be work and shelter there, no-one would know her, she could start again, she could clean and work in a house, she could serve in a tavern, she felt the tightly wrapped body warmth of the baby pressed close, she could, yes...she would even do that…whatever it would take to keep the child safe.

If only she had planned, taken more food, warmer clothes, but there had been no time. She was still in a state of shock after her sudden escape and the relief of her freedom mixed with the horror of what had happened and of what she had done to Anne. "Dear God" she pleaded, "Please let her be not too harmed, let her be alive."

She was tired, so very tired. The events of the day that had now passed seemed unbelievable. She was seventeen years old and yet it felt as if she had already had a lifetime of pain, and even the future held nothing for her except hardship and fear. She knew that she would have to stop and rest for a while, even perhaps sleep, if only for an hour or two. The night would pass and she could be early on the road towards Exeter, perhaps even towards safety. She tried to think, to plan, but her mind kept going back to the sight of Anne laying motionless on the floor with blood seeping from her head. What if she had killed her. She knew with a chilling certainty what that would mean for her, but what would happen to her baby. She stopped for a few moments to catch her breath and try and make a decision.

If she continued walking on through the night she would be that much nearer to Exeter and the chance of escape, but if she could only rest for a while then surely she would gain some more strength to help her continue. As she tried to follow the track that was becoming ever harder to see she came to the brow of a hill. Ahead and a little way off she saw an area of woodland. Straight ahead the way looked ever darker, more difficult and barren, but the fir trees, even in this season still full of leaf, holding out against the harsh winter gave Martha a strange sense of hope and seemed to offer some sort of shelter so she came off the track and made towards them. A few minutes later she came under their cover and immediately felt that she'd made the right decision as she found a small clearing where at least there seemed to be some shelter from the biting wind.

She slowly lowered herself against the trunk of a tree and opening her shawl looked down at the baby. She had managed at least to keep it warm and protected from the snow and the cold of the night. Amazingly it was sleeping peacefully. Martha gently stroked its head. She looked back at the way she had come and knew that she could not be seen from the track so any pursuers would probably not bother to come into the woods. She held the baby closer to her and snuggled deeper into her cloak. For a few beautiful moments she felt warm and somehow safe, surely a short sleep could do no harm, no harm at all...

…...............................

She awoke with a sudden start to the sound of the baby crying out its hunger. How long had she slept? There was no way to know as the sky through the covering of trees was still dark. While she'd slept the snow had continued to fall so that the way back to the track was not clear. Perhaps, she thought, in a moment of hope, that was for the better as it would make it harder for anyone following her. She put the baby to her breast and let it hungrily feed. She closed her eyes feeling the wonder and joy of the bond between them, and as the baby sucked and though she knew not where the words came from, Martha softly sang a lullabye

"Rest be inside you, Sleep now in safety
Peace be around you, You will always be mine."

The baby looked up at her. Calmly...trustingly. It was a single moment of happiness and Martha's only wish was that it could last forever, but then like a wave suddenly flooding over her she remembered the terrible events of the night before, and with them the knowledge…

The Witchfinder was coming.

1.
Martha

May 1603.

She was a strange child though no one could really say why. There had always been a self contained separateness about her that people said was unnatural. When she did smile, which was not often, it was as if it were to herself and to something secret and held within. There was a certain way that she looked at you when spoken to, an expression in her eyes that were made darker and accentuated by the ivory paleness of her skin, and then there was her hair which was of a lustrous, almost unnatural blackness, like the colour of the sky on the night she had come into the world.

She had been born eleven years before in the late autumn during the worst storm that anyone in the village could ever recall. The sky had been clawed with ragged streaks of lightning and filled with the sounds of torrential rain and thunder, but over and above all had been the pitiful screams of Elizabeth her mother as she struggled and fought to give birth. Sheltered in their homes, some had prayed for the woman desperately trying to bring a new life into the world and others had looked out as black clouds covered the fullness of the moon and spoken of darker things…of omens.

Inside the small cottage Goodwife Mary White who in her time had brought many of those in the village into the world and who knew from her experience that this birthing was not going well, sat by the side of the young woman trying to calm her whilst wiping the sweat from her frightened face. Huddled in the far corner, terrified and silent, a small eight year old boy watched as his mother screamed and writhed in agony, the light from the fire and a few candles throwing wild and strange shadows against the rough walls. He looked helplessly towards where his father John lay in a semi drunken stupor. He wanted to run from the cottage, away from everything, but felt unable even to stand up. He knew that he had to stay. To see. To witness.

Eventually as the first weak light of the early dawn came through the winding narrow lanes of the village, the storm passed away and with it also the terrible sounds that had come from the cottage. There were a few moments of absolute quiet, a silence that caused villagers, safe within their own cottages and relieved at the passing of the storm, to look to each other knowing that the departing night had also taken a young mother's soul.
And then, into that empty silence, there came the pitiful cry of a new born child.
That was Martha's birth.

Goodwife Mary gently wrapped the baby in a blanket, looked across the room to where John still lay insensible and turned towards the young boy. He did not have to be told that what she held in her arms had taken his mother's life. Mary moved towards him, her face clouded with sorrow and her voice soft .

"I am sorry for your loss Jared. There was nothing that could be done. Your mother is with God and his angels now, and this..." she held the baby closer to him "This is the new life she brought into the world. This is your sister."

The boy looked across at his father and then towards the bloodied and crumpled bed where his mother lay, her face already seeming changed and different in a way he found it impossible to understand. There was an expression of quiet peace there, but above all else there was a terrible and final stillness.

He was eight years old and knew two things with a sudden certainty. The first was that the memory of the night that had passed and the sight of his mother suffering on that bed of death would never leave him. The second was that he hated the baby that Goodwife Mary cradled in her arms, and he would always hate her.

He suddenly now found the strength and will to move that he had lacked for all of the long and terrible night. He knew that he had to get away from that room and the sight it held. He turned away and rushed out of the cottage into the empty streets and the chill of the early morning.

Later that day when John had sobered a little and villagers had come to help with all that had to be done, a search was made for the missing boy. He was finally found a mile from the village by the river bank, hunched over and staring at the fast flowing water. His face was red raw and tear stained and he would not, or could not speak. He was taken back to Goodwife Mary's cottage where he stayed for two days until after his mother's burial. Throughout all that time he remained mute. There were no more tears, nor were there questions, nothing but an empty frozen silence that led some to think the child had taken leave of his senses.

2
To Fly.

July 1603

Sometimes grief and the pain of loss passes. New lives are made, different directions taken. The years can bring relief and acceptance, or they can just move by, their seasons filled with nothing but regrets.

The house was a house of sorrow. Martha's father John, drank more, and was able to work less. Though a child, Martha understood that her father could hardly bear to look at her, seeing only the cause of his wife's death, but even that neglect and indifference was better than the spitefulness and outright hostility of her brother Jared, who seldom missed any chance to hurt her either with words or his rough hands.

Despite this, though whether by nature or more from a wish to stay out of trouble and harms way, she was a good child, obedient and helpful, and by the time she was in her eleventh year it was obvious that she would be a beauty. And yet, all were agreed…she was a strange child. She seemed to be able to bond with the animals of the village, the dogs, the horses and cows, even with the chickens, easier than with the other children. And for herself, she felt, she knew, that she was different. She had no friends, nor did she seem to want or need them. The games that the children of the village played, their friendships, their petty arguments and alliances held no interest for her. She seemed able to always have some part of her that was secret and contained, as if whatever went on around her, her father's constant drunkenness, Jared's almost continual cruelties, the daily life of the village, all these were outside her.

There were pleasures too. The beauty she saw whenever her chores were done and she had time to herself, just simply to be able to look up into the sky and watch the easy soaring flight of the birds. She wondered how far they traveled, where they came from and where they went to. She envied them that wonderful freedom, and she sometimes wondered what freedom and happiness was, and if when she grew up she would ever have it. Yes, that was it. The other children only wanted to grow, to live their lives, to work, to marry, and then to have children of their own.

Martha...she wanted to fly.

3
The Bird

The village of Clanton nestled deep in the Devonshire countryside enclosed and surrounded by thickly wooded hills and valleys. The river Coly ran through the outskirts of the village, flowing underneath an old stone bridge. A hard day's ride away to the west there lay the ancient City of Exeter, though few from the village had ever been there, the furthest that most had known was the market town of Honiton which lay seven miles away. To the south lay the hills which led to the steep and jagged cliffs that rose above the sea at Branscombe.

There had been a village here since earliest times and though country life was often hard and uncertain, the village itself was well ordered and was a bustling and self-contained community supporting a variety of trades. There was a forge, a mill, a tannery known throughout the county for the quality of its leather goods. There were a few small shops, a bakery, a butchers, wool workers, candle makers and many other small trades that were for the most part family run businesses. The farms and smallholdings that surrounded the village also provided work for the villagers.

The narrow lanes spread outwards from the square at the centre of the village. On one side of the square was the inn, which in many ways was the main social gathering place and heart of Clanton.

On the other side of the square was the village meeting house. At the corner was a small one cell lock-up. A winding lane led down to the largest building of all, the ancient church with its imposing tower that overlooked the village. For the most part the houses and cottages were of stone with thatched roofs though there were a few more substantial houses owned by some of the more prosperous local farmers and merchants.
A little way out of the village there was a track that led through some fields and a small wood before coming to where the river widened and deepened as it flowed away towards the sea.

On a beautiful cloudless day in the summer of that, her eleventh year, Martha was sitting in the house mending an old and torn shift when she heard laughter and shouting. She went to the window and looked outside to where Jared and three of his friends were throwing stones upwards towards a nest in a tree, each one taking it in turns to try and hit it. A sudden yell of success as the stone thrown by Jared found its mark and the nest came falling through the branches and to the ground. She rushed out of the cottage and over to where the young men were standing around a small black fledgling that was laying helplessly on the ground. She quickly darted between them bending down to pick it up and giving a small gasp as she saw that it was still alive.
As Jared and the others started to move towards her and for reasons she herself could not explain or understand, rather than holding it close to shelter

and protect it, instead she gently kissed the bird and with outstretched arms lifted it into the air, where it flew upwards out of Jared's reach. His face reddened with anger as he grabbed hold of Martha and slapped her across the face.
"That's what you get for stopping our sport."
Martha was used to Jared's anger and his ready use of his hands, but the suddenness and sting of his slap made her gasp and blink back the tears.
"It's not sport, it's just being cruel." Martha answered.
Jared smiled. "Yes I know it is "
For a moment she was taken by surprise by his answer and then without warning he punched her in the stomach. She doubled over and fell to the ground as around her Jared and his friends Edward, Ralph and Thomas started laughing.
Jared looked down at her, "But the thing is...I like being cruel."

She lay where she had fallen trying to get her breath back and watched as Jared and the others began to move off still laughing. She tried to get to her feet, but the pain of Jared's blow made her feel sick and she stayed where she was with her eyes squeezed shut. She heard a sound, and opening them she saw that on the ground next to her was the small bird that she had saved. She looked around in case Jared and the others would come back, but there was no one else in sight. She looked at the bird again. It had moved closer and was only inches from her face and somehow seemed to be studying her with its blue grey eyes. She found that she was able to smile, "Well little friend, it was worth what Jared did to me if it helped you to escape."

Martha began to stand up and was surprised to realize that the pain in her stomach had disappeared. She held out a hand and without hesitation the bird flew into her outstretched open palm. A strange and comforting warmth seemed to flow through her body and as she slowly moved towards and into the house, the bird remaining settled in her hand. On a shelf there were a few crusts from a loaf. She let the bird down next to them and watched as it pecked at them. Suddenly she heard the sounds of Jared and the others returning. She opened her hand and as if it understood the coming danger, the bird hopped into it. Martha moved away from the door and towards the window. She leaned closer and whispered "Fly away now…be safe"
It seemed to her as if the bird understood her words. It looked directly at her for a moment and then flew away. She watched with envy as it took to the sky wishing only that she could follow it.

That night, laying in her bed in the far corner of the cottage and unable to sleep, Martha thought back on the day. She had always felt a closeness to animals, some sort of understanding that she'd never found either at home or with the other children of the village, but there had been something very different in the feeling she had had for that small and seemingly helpless bird. There was something she could neither describe nor explain about the way it had looked at her when she was laying on the ground after Jared's punch, and also about the way the pain of that blow had vanished unlike any of her past experiences of Jared's beatings. She wondered if she would ever see it again. She knew without a doubt that if she did, then she would know it…and it would know her.

The next day she received the answer to her previous night's thoughts, when only a few minutes after Jared and her father had set off to Honiton market, with their cart laden with various goods from some of the traders in the village, and at the same window from which she had urged it to fly away she looked and saw it patiently sitting. Once again she tentatively held out her open hand towards it and again it flew down into her palm, settling there as she moved to the shelf and took a few crumbs into her other hand. The bird hopped from one hand to the other and ate the offered food. Once again she felt the warmth that she had experienced the day before. Martha looked at it. Its feathered coat was black with almost a bluish tinge to it and as before, the bird seemed almost enquiringly to be returning her gaze. "I want to give you a name" she said softly, and then thinking for a few moments it suddenly became obvious what that name would be…the name of the mother she had never known, the mother who had died bringing her into the world. "I shall call you Beth." She gently stroked the small bird and lifted it to the window "Fly now, but please, if you can, if you want...be my friend, come to me every day"

And so it was. As if the bird had understood and agreed, it became a daily event. It became the time she looked forward to as she woke each morning and as she did all her household work and it was the time she looked back on as she lay in her bed at night. It was the time she thought about when her father angrily shouted at her and when Jared mistreated and hit her. There was never a set hour, which made it all the more special when Beth suddenly appeared, although it was always and only when Martha was on her own and neither her father or Jared were around. It no longer seemed to matter that she had no friends or that her father was indifferent to her and that Jared was cruel and spiteful. She had Beth, and she had come to know for the first time in her young life what true happiness was.

4
Beth.

October 1603

The summer turned to autumn and she wondered whether a time would come when Beth would no longer appear at the window. She knew that there was nothing she could do if that day ever came but she did know how she would feel. It was as if her life had been in two parts, the one before Beth that had been loneliness, and what she had known since that day when she had picked the small bird up from the ground and saved it from Jared and his friends.

It was the late afternoon of a blustery October day. The leaves that had fallen from the trees swirled as gusts of wind blew and scattered them through the lanes. Martha had finished all the work and had set the broth to cook in the cauldron over the fire and still Beth had not appeared. Neither had her father, who she knew from experience would be slowly getting more and more drunk at the inn. She wondered whether she should ask Jared who had gone to collect some wood for the fire to go and fetch him and then decided it were best not to ask him anything, but just to patiently wait. She felt worried that her friend, her only friend, had not come, perhaps there was a good reason, perhaps…
The harsh voice of Jared cut through her thoughts.
"Martha "
She turned towards the cottage door, to where he

stood just outside.

"Martha." she heard Jared call to her again but this time there was something in the tone of his voice that sent a chill through her. She walked towards the doorway and as she did so Jared roughly pushed past her into the cottage. As he came inside, she could see that he was holding a piece of netting and within it grasping something within his hands. She looked from his hands to his face and immediately his cruel smile told her all she needed to know. He slowly opened his hands and she stared in horror at Beth laying helplessly there entangled inside the net with one of its wings hanging loosely down. She felt a cold shudder run through her body.

"What have you done ?"

Jared laughed, "I wanted to see if it could fly as well with one wing as with two."

"Please don't harm it" Martha desperately pleaded "Give it to me so that I can see, so that I can help it"

"Did you think I hadn't noticed your little friend. Your little plaything coming all the time." He held it tauntingly towards her.

"Jared, if you dare do any more harm to it…"

"And what can you do little sister" he sneered "You be as weak as this bird and I could snap its neck just as easy as I could yours"

"Why Jared, why would you do that ?"

"Because I can, and because I want to." The look on his face turned from anger and contempt to hate. " I can kill this creature just as easy as you did kill our mother"

Again. The accusation, the taunt that had filled her entire childhood. How many times did she have to say the answer.

"I did not kill her. She died in giving me life."

"So it was her life in exchange for yours, you little witch." Jared began to grow flushed and his voice became angrier. "Even now I can remember her screams, better you had died than her."

He moved slowly and threateningly towards her and she stepped backwards suddenly aware of the heat of the fire behind her where the cauldron was hanging. She looked up at Jared and saw in his eyes that there were no words she could say that would make him stop. They both stood there for a few moments, the only sounds in the room now being the pathetic sounds coming from the injured bird grasped in Jared's rough hands and the crackle of the fire and the bubbling of the broth in the cauldron.

Martha felt a desperation that overwhelmed her. She knew that there was nothing that she could say or do to make Jared stop. He looked down at the bird in his hands and smiled. "I think it now be time to break the other wing"

Suddenly it was as if something in her had taken over and her body was acting and moving without her will. She turned around and seized the ladle that lay at the side, thrust it into the boiling broth and hurled it at Jared's face.

 He immediately dropped the bird and raised his hands to cover his eyes and protect himself but was too late to stop the scalding liquid striking him. He screamed and fell to the floor where he lay writhing in agony. Martha looked to where he had dropped the bird. She knew that she had to find it before Jared recovered as he now surely would kill it. As for her, she didn't care what her punishment would be as long as she could save Beth. She looked all around the floor but could not see it. Meanwhile Jared had staggered to his feet still clutching at his face

"You bitch…you demon …you've blinded me. I'll kill you for this"

She wanted to run but knew she had to find Beth first… surely it could not have gone very far with its broken wing. Suddenly she heard a sound other than Jared's moaning. She looked up from the floor to the window ledge and there it was. For a moment her mind could not believe what she was seeing. How could the bird have freed itself from the netting and got to the ledge when it had a broken wing? She moved towards it with her hand outstretched and was within a few inches when she felt her head suddenly jerked backwards as Jared had reached her and grabbed her by the hair. Her head seemed to explode as he brought his hand down hard against her ear and dragged her back from the ledge. It was not the beating that she knew was coming that filled her with fear, but the knowledge of what Jared would then do to the bird. She looked again to the window ledge and watched in amazement as Beth first seemed to look straight at her and into her eyes before turning around and with a flurry of its small wings lifted into the air and flew away.

Though Jared had beaten her more times than she could remember she knew that this time he would do far worse and somehow this knowledge gave her the courage to reach up and claw her nails across his already scalded and damaged face. He gave a savage shout of pain and released his hold on her hair to clutch at his face. The moment was enough for Martha to run to the door and out into the street. She looked around uncertain what to do next or where to go to escape from him. She began to run through the winding lanes of the village and towards the church. As she ran she kept looking behind to see if he was pursuing her but the lanes were empty. She reached the church and lifting the latch on the door stepped inside. Catching her breath she allowed the stillness and quiet to envelop her. All at once the fear seemed to leave her and she felt a sense of peace and even security. She tried to get her thoughts in order. She knew that she'd hurt Jared and that there would be a punishment, but what did that matter…Beth had somehow escaped and was safe.

5
Sanctuary

The Church had always been there, a part of the very life of the village. It had been built hundreds of years before in the reign of a long dead King and was named for St Andrew. It could be seen from miles around the village. The tower with its unusual six sided shape surmounted by a weather vane in the shape of a golden cockerel, held within it eight bells that summoned the villagers to prayer and also rang out at other times, the joyous peals at weddings and the solitary and muffled ring at burials.

In the old graveyard that surrounded the church lay the body of Martha's mother. There were times when she had stood by the side of that grave, marked as it was by a simple wooden cross with the name Elizabeth carved onto it and had wondered what she had been like. Would the life that she knew have been different had her mother lived? Would her father not be a broken and drunk man, would Jared have been kind to her, even friendly? All unknowable questions. Her life was what it was.

She had rushed quickly through that graveyard and entered the church, which at that time of day was completely empty. She moved down the nave towards the altar as if drawn towards it by a promise of sanctuary and safety. She had known this church all of her life, being brought to it from her youngest days. Though she did not understand much of what was said and done during the services, she always felt a sense of peace and security in it, so unlike many of the other village children who fidgeted restlessly wanting only for the service and sermon to be over. Her thoughts, and the peaceful silence were interrupted as the door was suddenly flung open and she saw her father standing there with Jared at his side, blood still running down the side of his face. She looked round hopelessly seeking a way to escape and realizing that there was none she stood still as they both moved towards her. Jared started to come ahead but her father grabbed him by the arm. "You leave this to me boy"

She looked from one to the other, from Jared's hatred and rage to her father's drunken anger. She closed her eyes and waited for them to reach her and for the first blow to fall.

A sudden shout. "Stop. There will be no violence in God's house".

It was the voice of Henry Wilkin the priest, who hearing the raised voices had come out of the vestry and into the church.

Martha breathed a momentary sigh of relief. She pleadingly looked towards him hoping against hope for some kind of intercession and help.

"John Carter, if you need to chastise your child then you do it in your own house and not here."

Her father turned and pointed at Jared who stood by his side, holding a blood-soaked rag to his injured face.

"Look at what she's done. Do you not think she deserves to be punished?"

The priest looked from one to the other and then at Martha.

"That's for you to decide…but it will not happen here."
Martha's father stepped forward and grasped her by the arm and pulled her back towards the door. She twisted away from him and ran back up the aisle towards the altar where the priest was standing. She looked up into his face, searching for any sign of compassion and understanding but finding only a look of indifference.
She tried to explain. "Please. Jared was hurting my bird. He was going to…"
The look on Wilkin's face became one of annoyance as he called to Martha's father "Take your child and do what you will" and turned away and began walking back towards the vestry.
Martha knew then that it would be easier to submit to whatever was going to happen than to resist, and so she walked back towards the door where her father seized her by the collar of her shift and angrily pulled her outside.

The walk back to their house though taking only a few minutes seemed to be happening in a sort of slow motion. By this time a few people had gathered outside their houses to see what all the fuss was about, and Martha would always remember how the onlookers had watched the little procession as her father walked back towards their cottage roughly dragging Martha along followed by a moaning Jared still clutching the rag to his face. Worst of all were the faces of the village children laughing and smirking at what they knew was going to happen to her very soon.

That night as Martha lay in her bed, every single movement making her wince from the bruises of the savage beating she'd received, above all else was the feeling of relief that somehow, though she knew not how, Beth had managed to miraculously escape, even with a wing that had looked to be broken and useless.

For the next few days Martha lived with the fear that Jared was only waiting for the chance to revenge himself. The bruises from her beating were beginning to fade but it was obvious that Jared would be marked for the rest of his life. The skin on the side of his face was red and blistered and running through the disfigurement was a crooked scar where her nails had clawed at him.
Though she had hoped against hope that Beth might return, as days and then weeks passed, Martha came to accept that it was not going to happen.
Sometimes she thought that it would have been impossible for the bird to survive with its broken wing and that it probably would have died. But there were also times when she closed her eyes and saw once again that last sight of Beth where having hopped on to the window ledge it had turned to look at her before flying away. She also consoled herself with the thought that at least Jared had not been able to finish what he had started and managed to kill the bird.
And weeks and months became seasons.

6
Margaret

1606.

And the seasons became years.
King James had brought a new and, in many ways, a very different governance to the country. The early enthusiasm that had greeted a younger and male Monarch after fifty years of being ruled by women gradually melted away as the extravagance and richness of the life at his court became more generally known. There were other things that also were spoken of, his lack of interest in matters of state, his obsession with hunting, and, though it was only ever mentioned in whispers, the talk of his closeness to a succession of young male favorites. He had become less tolerant of those of his subjects who favored and still clung to the old religion and felt that their first loyalty was to the Pope and the Church of Rome, the more so after the failed gunpowder plot against his life in the November of the previous year.
His main passion though had remained constant, the campaign against witchcraft and those evil and secret practitioners who with their spells and incantations were even more dangerous than any others who could threaten his Kingdom.

In the village of Clanton as in so many other places, life continued as it always had and as it surely always would. Martha continued to grow, her life unchanging in its daily work and Jared continued to hate her. Their father John took more and more to drink and as everyone had predicted came the day when after a particularly heavy bout of drinking, he fell from the cart and broke his leg. William the carpenter made him a crutch of sorts but though able to hobble about with its help, he effectively ceased to be of any use as far as work went and spent more and more time just sitting in the cottage where it fell to Martha to care for any of his needs. For Jared, now having to do all the carter's work on his own, his father just became one more thing in his life that gave him a continual reason for anger, which more often than not came to be vented on Martha.

Ever since childhood Martha had been fascinated by the natural world around her and had developed an interest in the uses that the flowers and herbs she so loved could be put to. It had started one day when she had gone for a walk and seen old Margaret Woodson picking some flowers at the edge of the village. She seemed to be choosing them carefully and Martha had watched her for a while not wanting to disturb her. Margaret had looked up and smiled at her.
"Does ee want to know what I do child?"
Martha had nodded and moved closer. Margaret showed her the flower that she held in her hand.
"These be marshmallow, an' they be good for sore throats. She pointed down at a wicker basket at her feet. "And they be elderflower which do be good for fevers"
Martha bent down and looked at the various flowers

in the basket.

Sensing the girl's interest and attention Margaret asked her. "Does ee want to learn of these things?" Martha nodded. She was so used to her father's orders and Jared's anger that she found it hard to think that someone would show her kindness and offer to teach her anything.

"Then come to me any time you want." She pointed down the track that led out of the village towards a small and tumble-down cottage that stood apart from any others. Its thatched roof was patched and threadbare and Martha could see that the walls were cracked.

Margaret smiled. "I know it don't seem much, but it be just like a person."

Martha looked at her with a quizzical expression, not understanding what the old woman meant. She looked into her eyes and saw them twinkle with amusement. "It do not matter what be on the outside" Margaret explained. "It's what be inside that does."

…...............................

And Martha did go to the cottage the first chance she had to have some time of her own. She gently knocked on the door and heard a voice from inside calling out. "Come in child."

She pushed the door open and stepped inside at the same time wondering how the old woman had known it was her. She looked around realising that this cottage was unlike her own home or any other she had ever been in.

Hanging from the beams there were many bunches of dried flowers and herbs, giving off a sweet aroma. On a shelf against the wall were a collection of bottles containing different coloured liquids. There was a table in the middle of the room with mixing bowls and a few large spoons. In the far corner was a small bed.

Margaret was sitting in the corner by the window and got up to welcome Martha with open arms and an embrace that suddenly made Martha realise with a shock that no one had ever done this to her before.

The next couple of hours seemed to race as Margaret explained what was in some of the jars and bottles and how they were measured into the mixing bowls to produce different remedies, and what conditions and sicknesses they could be used to help. Martha was fascinated and wished she could stay even longer, but finally Margaret looked out of the window and said. "You best be a goin' now afore it get dark."

Seeing the look of disappointment that passed across Martha's face she quickly
added "Remember...this be a place you can always come. Here you will always be welcome."

Martha closed the door behind her and stepped out into the lane. She did not know how long she had been with Margaret. There had been so much to see and so many questions she had asked, all of which the old woman had tried to answer clearly and patiently.

As she walked back towards her own house her mind was full of her visit, though she instinctively knew that it was something that was for herself alone and not to be shared with anyone else.

And Martha did go again and was again made welcome. Any time she could get away from her father and whenever Jared was away working or at the inn drinking with his friends, she went to visit old Margaret. Each time she came away she felt that she had learned something new. Little by little Margaret taught her all about the herbs and potions that she had found so strange and yet so interesting ever since she had first stepped into what for everyone else in the village would be just a broken down old cottage but for Martha was a magical place of wonder.
There were also times when they would just sit and talk. Martha felt that she could tell Margaret anything and she told of the life she had at home and of the things that she felt inside.

One day as they were talking, Martha felt that she wanted to speak about Beth. She somehow felt that Margaret would understand the feelings she had had for the bird.
"There was a bird that I saved from my brother Jared. He had broken its wing and yet somehow it managed to fly away. I don't know how. It seemed to be so hurt and yet when I held it in my hands it was as if..." Martha stopped, unsure of whether to tell of what she had always thought and yet never told of for fear that it would seem unbelievable. Margaret looked at Martha and spoke softly. "Go on child."
"It was as if my holding it had made it better."

Margaret nodded "All in the village do know of your brother and his temper, and as to the bird, there be many things under heaven that folks don't be knowin' of."

Margaret looked intently into Martha's eyes as if searching or perhaps trying to understand something.

"Let me look at your hands child."

Martha held out her hands towards Margaret who took them into her own which were spotted and gnarled with veins.

"What are those marks?" asked Martha innocently.

Margaret smiled "They be the marks of age my dear. One day, long into the years to come you'll have them too." Margaret paused and moved Martha's hands closer to her face. Her expression seemed to change as she ran her old crooked fingers along the lines in Martha's palms.

Martha noticed it and asked, "Is there anything that troubles you?"

Margaret was silent for a few moments and then brought Martha's hands to her face and gently kissed them. She looked down and smiled again, though this time Martha somehow sensed an unspoken sadness behind that smile.

"There be nothin' child. Nothin' at all."

7
Anne.

For Jared, there had been few young women of the village who were interested in him. They all knew of his foul temper and sudden rages. Also his face, never handsome, now was further marked by the disfigurement of the burn and scar on its side, but he had met a woman, Anne, from a village a couple of miles away. She was older than Jared and indeed being approaching thirty and having a plain face and generally unattractive bearing and manner seemed not to care about either Jared's looks or his all too obvious nature as she was only too aware of the passing of time and also of her lessening chances of finding anyone better, if at all, and so they were married with Anne coming to live with Jared, his crippled father and Martha.

From the beginning it became obvious to Martha that Anne could give as well as she received and with her quick temper and sharp tongue was more than a match for Jared. When there were arguments Martha very soon became aware that more often than not, it was Anne who got the better of them and as time passed she was also painfully aware that after coming off worse in a confrontation with Anne it would only mean more trouble for her. As for Anne, there were times when she treated Martha kindly and well, often intervening to stop Jared's ill treatment of her but there were also other times when Martha either caught the sharp end of Anne's temper or saw her turn away when Jared wanted to vent his anger on her.

Whenever there was no more work to be done, Martha would try and spend as much time as possible with old Margaret. Her tiny run-down cottage at the very edge of the village became more of a home to her than her own. She gradually learned more about herbs and wild flowers and the uses to which they could be put to ease and cure illnesses. Sometimes she would accompany Margaret when she visited someone who was sick and in need of treatment. The villagers became used to seeing the two of them together and would sometimes joke about their relationship. That mattered to neither of them as Margaret was past caring what others thought and Martha neither having or wanting friends of her own age among the village children also cared not.

And more seasons came and went....and more years. And in those years Martha's father John died, was buried in the churchyard next to her mother, and was neither mourned nor missed by anyone, not by Jared and Anne for whom he had become just a useless mouth to feed, nor by Martha who had only ever known coldness, drunkenness and indifference.

For Martha the only loss that had mattered had been Margaret.
In a hard winter she had caught what at first had seemed to be just a chill. Martha had spent as much time as she was allowed to tend her, but despite everything, the infection went to her chest and

within a few days it was obvious that the end was very near. On what was to be the last time Martha was with her, the old woman wanted only for her to sit by her bedside and hold her hand. Margaret saw the fear in Martha's eyes and quietly said "Don't you be afeared girl. This be natural and only a goin from one way of bein' to another."

"But is there nothing that can help? Are there no herbs or potions?" Martha asked anxiously.

Margaret smiled. "There can be none that help when God do call for you. I've had my years. I've had my joys and also my sorrows and now it do be time."

Martha felt herself being drawn into Margaret's calm acceptance and gently squeezed her hand. Suddenly she saw a look of concern cross the old woman's face. "Your child years are passed and you be growing to a young woman now. You have the special gift of healing in your hands and in your spirit. I knew it the first time I met you, but you must always be careful."

"Be careful of what?" asked Martha.

"Of them that are feared of anything they don't understand. Of them that envy your gift...of them that be scared of it."

"Why should that be?" said Martha. "Any cures I can do are what you have taught me, and all come from nature, and any gifts that I have I would use only for good."

Margaret closed her eyes and remained silent for a few moments. When she opened them Martha could see that they were brimming with tears. "Child...I am tired. Go now. I must sleep".

Martha nodded and pulling the rough blanket up around Margaret to protect her better against the cold, she slowly bent down and gently kissed the old woman on the forehead.

As she reached the doorway of the tiny cottage Martha turned and looked back to the far corner of the room where Margaret lay on the bed.

"I will come tomorrow to see how you are". She said.

But the next day when Martha came towards the edge of the village, she saw with a sudden rush of fear that there were a few people standing outside the cottage. She ran forward and saw Henry Wilkin in his black gown coming out of the door talking with one of the church wardens. She rushed up to them. "Has Margaret asked for you?" she asked breathlessly.

Wilkin turned towards her with obvious annoyance at having been interrupted. "Not that it's any of your business but Margaret is past calling for me or anyone else. Now be gone, we have a burying to arrange."

Martha wanted to go inside and say her own goodbye to Margaret but Wilkin and the warden stood firmly in her way. She could see from Wilkin's face that his annoyance was turning to anger, so she turned around and slowly walked home knowing that she had lost her only friend and also part of her life.

In the days that followed, Martha felt a strange

sense of unreality at the knowledge that she would never see Margaret again. At night when she went to bed she fell into her sleep with a deep sense of sadness and in the morning when she woke there were those few moments when she was eager to start her housework so as to be free to visit the old cottage at the edge of the village that had become more of a home to her than her own. All too soon she remembered that Margaret was gone and then with an aching emptiness inside her she got out of her bed and began the day.

There were times after her death when villagers who had previously asked Margaret for help and healing, wanted the same from Martha despite her young age. At first, she had not wanted to but little by little she started to offer small assistance to some of the villagers, making and setting a poultice on a boil, mixing a herbal remedy to settle stomach cramps, making a lotion that would ease aching joints. She felt that each time she helped someone or cured their pains it was an act of remembrance to the old woman who had come to mean so much to her. For her part, Anne seemed not to care as long as all the housework that Martha was responsible for was completed and for his part Jared was happy to have her out of sight.

8
Matthew.

May 1608

Jared had not wanted to take Martha to market with him. He was happiest just going either on his own or when they were not at their own work, with Edward, Ralph or Thomas, and if the day had gone well, and sometimes even if it hadn't, he could take a jar of ale with them or some of the other traders. For whatever reasons of her own though, Anne had been insistent and whatever else, he knew and sullenly admitted to himself that arguments would make no difference and would indeed only serve to make her tongue sharper and her temper fouler.
They set out early for the trip to market. Jared sat silently as they drove, and Martha was more than happy for that. For her, who in all of her sixteen years had seldom been far outside the village even the commonplace sights and sounds of the early morning countryside around them were interesting as they made their way towards market.
Eventually after an hour or so they came to the crest of the final hill from which they could see the town laid out below them and began their descent down the steep and winding road.

The town of Honiton had been granted its market charter long ago in the reign of Henry lll and in this part of the county of Devonshire it was by far the most important. As they came into the town with its long straight and wide street that ran down through the centre and up the hill at the other end, Martha looked around at the busy and bustling scene as traders were unloading their carts and setting up the stalls to display and hopefully sell their wares. They reached the part where Jared usually took a place and still without a word, he halted the horse and got down. Martha knew that he had not wanted to take her with him and so thought it best just to sit quietly until told to do otherwise. A few local traders greeted Jared in passing also looking up to where she still sat on the cart. She saw one of them lean towards Jared and make some remark which caused him to scowl and for the man to walk off laughing.

Finally Martha called out to Jared. "Is there any help that I can be giving you?"

"And what help could you ever be" he answered sullenly "I know what I'm about and I've always managed on my own."

"May I get down and perhaps have a short walk to look around the market? " she asked tentatively.

"Do what you like just don't be too long about it." With a sudden rush of a feeling of freedom Martha climbed down from the cart and began to move away before Jared had a chance to reconsider and change his mind. She walked a few paces along the high street casually looking at the different things on offer and for sale. Apart from the normal market vegetables and poultry there were stalls selling leather goods and shoes, pots and pans, small pieces of furniture and of course the lace for which Honiton was famed throughout the land.

She came to a stall on the other side of the road where a young man was setting out various pieces of pottery. There were jugs and platters, mugs and bowls of the usual kind to be found in every house but there were also some others, all with a more interesting design and with a distinctive glaze and decoration. They carried pictures of small animals, of flowers, trees and of birds.
Martha picked up a small round dish and saw with a sudden start that the engraved design on it was that of a young raven with outstretched wings looking as if ready to take flight. Her mind immediately went back to when she had cradled the bird she had named Beth in her hands all those years before and of how she had saved it from Jared's cruelty. She examined it, turning it around in her hands and remembering that time both with pleasure and yet also with a sense of loss. She became aware that the young man who had been busying himself setting up his stall had now stopped, and looking up from what he was doing, caught her eye and smiled.
"Good day. Is there something I can show to you" He looked at the dish Martha was holding "or perhaps even sell to you ?" he added.
Martha put the piece down on the stall and smiled back at him feeling a little embarrassed and knowing that she had not a single coin of her own to spend even had she wanted to."Oh I'm not here to buy, I've also come to sell…we are across the market over there."
She nodded towards where she could see Jared with his head down as he laid out the various goods he

had brought to market.

"Well at least I think the weather is set fair for us" he replied.

"I hope so. This is my first time here, but I heard tell that at the last market it rained nearly all day."

"Well I'm new to this town and this is also my first time here."

Martha looked down again at the various pieces of pottery especially the few that were all so very different from the plain and ordinary things she was used to in her own home. She pointed at them "These ones seem very different to the others" she said, "They're very beautiful, especially this one with the bird on it…do you make them?"

"It feels like I've always been making them." he answered. " My father was a potter before me, and when he died my uncle took over his business and he lets me make some of my own designs."

Martha looked at him. He was not much older than her. He had dark brown and slightly curly hair and an open and kind face. There was something about him that seemed so very different from any of the young men of her own village.

Martha looked across the high street and saw that Jared was looking around for her. Though she would have liked to stay and talked more with the potter she also knew that it would not be good to give Jared any excuse for anger so early in the day.

"I must go now…I hope you have a very good day."

The young man smiled at her once more. "I would like to sell some of my pottery" he paused "But I have already had a good day."

Martha looked into his eyes which she noticed were dark like his hair and feeling herself beginning to blush and not knowing how or what to answer, just smiled and turned away back towards where Jared was waiting.

The morning passed with many lookers and thankfully also some customers.
Occasionally Martha would look across the crowded market street towards the stall of the young potter. He seemed to be doing good business and once she was sure she had seen him looking towards where she and Jared were, but she had quickly looked away, embarrassed to make any eye contact. She had enjoyed the few minutes they had spent talking and would have liked it to have been longer, but she hoped that he would have a good enough day to make him come again…perhaps even regularly.

9
The Fight

By mid-day the market was hot and full of people. Though he had a good thirst on him and would have rather gone to the ale house himself Jared knew he couldn't leave the horse and cart and his stall and so he'd given Martha a few coins and sent her to get him some ale. As the time passed he felt hotter and thirstier and was cursing her for the time it was taking, although some part of him realized that the taverns were bound to be full and busy. Finally he saw her and began to calm down anticipating the satisfaction the drink would bring.

Martha walked towards Jared with the large tankard of ale held tightly as she threaded her way through the market crowd. She had almost reached him when some young children running and laughing between the closely packed stalls bumped into her causing her to stumble and drop the tankard spilling its foaming contents onto the dusty street. In a moment, Jared had seized hold of her and was shaking her from side to side, his face red with anger. She tried to twist away from him, knowing only too well what would be coming next. He grabbed her by the hair and pulled her head back. "You stupid bitch...can't you..."

"Leave her be."
Without releasing his hold on Martha, Jared turned to see who had called out. From across the market he saw a young man looking towards him.

In response he tightened his grip on Martha's hair and with his other free hand he slapped her across the face. Within moments the young man had run across the road and with a single blow to Jared's cheek had knocked him to the ground.

Jared stared up in shock and then scrambled to his feet, glaring at his assailant.

"What has it to do with you" he angrily demanded, "She's here with me and I can do with her as I will".

"Not while I am here to stop you."

Jared took a moment to size up the person who had struck him. He was a little shorter than Jared and slightly built. It was only the surprise of the attack that had taken him off guard and he knew he was more than a match for the young man facing him. The disturbance had caused a small crowd to gather around them anticipating some further diversion from the usual market day proceedings. Jared was not going to leave things as they stood, he was going to have his revenge…and more. There was an uneasy silence for a few moments in which the young man had turned away from Jared and towards Martha who was backed against the cart where Jared's slap had knocked her.

"Are you all right?" he asked her, holding her by the shoulders.

Martha nodded and looked into the concerned face of the young potter. He wasn't smiling now but was looking directly into her eyes to make sure she had not been hurt. She felt a strange and comforting safety in the way he held her. She glanced to the side and her face froze into a look of fear as she saw Jared who had moved behind the young man and raised his fist. She opened her mouth to cry out a warning, but it was already too late. The young man crumpled to the ground as a sudden punch landed on the back of his head. As he tried to get up, a kick to his stomach from Jared took the breath out of him. He was aware of the girl running at the man and grabbing him by the arm to try and prevent another kick. It gave him the chance to get to his feet and though still winded, at least to be able to face up to his opponent.

The crowd had now grown and formed a circle around the two fighters who with fists now raised and clenched began warily to look for an opening in the others defense. Jared swung his arm round towards his opponent's head, but the young man was quicker and sidestepped while at the same time managing to land a well-placed blow against Jared's nose from which blood began to spurt. Jared tried to kick out against the other man's legs but instead lost his footing and stumbled forward, his head lowering down towards a fist that thudded into his face lifting him totally off balance and causing him to drop to his knees. He waited for the kicks that now he was down would probably start…but nothing came. The young man just remained standing above him waiting for him to rise to his feet and continue fighting. Jared knew he was beaten and yet felt unwilling and unable to walk away now that all these people were watching and shouting out for the continuation of the fight. With a sudden shout he sprang up and butted his head into the young man's midriff that was only a few inches away. Though his head made contact it was not with enough force to do any damage and in response another blow came down and caught him on the side of his face. He shakily stood up and began wildly lashing out in a frenzy with both arms, and though one or two of his blows landed they were all met with sharp and well-aimed punches in return. Jared could feel and taste the blood from his nose which was now mixing with that from the split lip that the last punch had caused. He knew he wanted it to end but knew also that he had to save face and go on. At that moment the market warden pushed angrily through the gathered crowd calling for the disturbance to stop.

There was a pause and the young potter caught the look that the man he had just beaten gave towards the girl and in turn saw the fear of reprisal in her eyes. He moved a step closer and said to him. "We'll fight no more, but you will come to this market again… as I will. If you harm her because of what has taken place today, you will regret it. Do you understand that?"
Jared knew the truth of what was being said and made no answer. The question was repeated as the young man took a step towards him. Jared quickly nodded and turned away.

The journey home was in silence. Martha had heard what had been said but still did not think it was within Jared's nature to accept it. She sat silent and tensed waiting for…would it be a beating…angry words…a threat? As they began to draw near to Clanton she looked across at Jared. He had wiped

away the blood on his face, but it was swollen and bruised with one eye puffed up and half closed. He felt her gaze on him and finally spoke "When Anne asks. It were men who tried to rob us " he paused "There were three of them" he would not look directly at her but continued to stare straight ahead at the track leading to the village. There was silence whilst she tried to think. If when questioned this one lie would save her from Jared's anger, then it was an easy decision to make.
"Do you understand." He still would not look at her for a response.
"I understand," she replied as the cart turned the final bend in the track towards home.

That night as she lay waiting for sleep to come Martha thought back on the day. She remembered the young potter and what had happened and how he had come to protect her from Jared. It was the very first time in all her life that anyone had stood up for her. She wondered whether she would ever again be taken to the market and if she were, then would she see him again. She thought about what he had said to Jared about harming her and whether his threat had been no more than words.

10
Meeting.

The next morning when she saw Jared, he seemed to look at her in a different way. His face was still swollen and there was a purple bruise around his eye, but Anne had been ready to accept the story he'd told. She had looked to Martha for confirmation as Jared had spoken of the attempt to rob them, and Martha had nodded her silent assent. After her chores had been done Martha asked Anne if she could go for a walk. Her mind was still so full of the previous day's events and she wanted to be alone to think about them. She remembered not just the fight, but of when she had spoken with the young man earlier in the day and what he'd said to her, and the way that he had looked at her.
She had walked a short way from the village and turned down towards the path that led to the river. She came to a small clearing when she suddenly stopped. There just a few feet in front of her was the young potter.

For a moment she was lost for words at the surprise of seeing him again. He had also stopped as he saw her They both stood silent for a few moments and then he smiled and moved towards her.
"Hello Martha "
"How is it that you know my name?" she asked puzzled.
 "Yesterday…in the market, after you had gone, I asked after you and where you were from."
"But how did you…why did you…?"

"I saw the way he looked at you and did not trust him to keep to his word" he answered with a look of concern. "I wanted to see if you were unharmed."
Martha smiled "He did keep to his word, though he made me tell that he had fought with three others."
They both laughed and then the young potter replied, "What matter if he said three or thirty three…as long as he did not harm you."
Martha looked at him "Yesterday, I did not get a chance to thank you…I did not even know your name."
"Matthew."
Martha looked at him and repeated his name. "Matthew. Thank you...but why did you get involved ?"
"Do you not remember, we had spoken a while before when you looked at my pots .."he paused " I liked you and saw the way you had kept glancing over to your own stall, I thought the man waiting might be your man."
" He's my brother Jared and I do live in his house with him and his wife Anne" Martha replied.
"I know, I asked others in the market more than just your name after you had left."
Martha looked down, feeling herself blushing.
"Is he always like that to you?"
Martha nodded "He is like that to everyone, but especially to me."
"Can you not leave?"
"I am but sixteen years old. Where could I go and what would I do?"
There being no answer to this, they were both silent for a few moments before Matthew spoke "May I

see you again?"
Martha looked into his face and smiled. "Yes...I would like that."
"Shall I come to your house? Perhaps I can make peace with your brother."
"No please do not " Martha replied quickly "Jared is not one who can forget or forgive, it would just cause trouble."
"I do not fear Jared and if he..."
"It is not only Jared; he has friends and they are very like him...please I would not want you to be..."

Matthew took her hands. "Martha, do not be upset, I understand. We can meet each other here in this place by the river. That way no one need know."
Martha immediately agreed. "This would be a wonderful place. It is where I often come to be on my own. She looked round at the clearing among the tall old trees and down towards where the river flowed a few paces away.
"I have always loved it here, there is something special about this place."
Matthew smiled "And surely our meeting here will only make it more so."
Martha nodded. "It will." She looked down realising that Matthew was still holding both her hands in his own. It felt so right, and it made her eyes begin to well up as she thought that this moment in all her sixteen years was the first time she could ever remember being touched with tenderness.
Matthew put a hand to her face and turned it towards his own. "Are you sad, is there something

wrong?"

Martha wanted to say that she somehow knew that with Matthew by her side, nothing would ever be wrong again. She wanted to say that although she had known him only since yesterday, she felt that it had been forever...and could be forever. She wanted to say so many things but didn't know the right words.

"No, nothing is wrong." she whispered.

The feeling of his hands, the touch against her cheek, these were wonderful new sensations. She had heard some of the village girls talk of such things, but when they spoke it had always seemed to her that they were to be shared, discussed, even laughed over, but she knew this to be different. She wanted no one else to know, she wanted this to be special. A secret.

"I must go back now " she said quietly beginning to turn away before Matthew could see the tears that she felt were coming.

"I will come here on Sunday " Matthew said, "Please meet me."

Martha nodded "I will try, I promise." she said as she started to move back towards the village.

Matthew let her go a few paces watching her and then called out," Martha."

She turned, no longer able to hold back the tears as he rushed towards her, and enfolding her in his arms, kissed her on her lips. She realised and knew without a doubt that everything that had gone before...the hurts, the loneliness, the indifference of her father, Jared's cruelties...all of these now belonged to a different time, and that she would remember this moment forever as marking the start of her real life. It was, in a strange way as if a line had been drawn. There had been the past...and now there was a future.

They moved apart. Martha felt that her entire being was somehow changed. How could it be...only an hour ago she had been a different person, alone, friendless, uncared for. She looked at Matthew and softly said." Yes. Sunday, at the mid-day."

He smiled and repeated her words. "Sunday. At mid-day."

She moved away and began to walk back to the village, knowing that he was watching her. As she reached a bend in the track she turned. He was there. He raised his arm in a farewell wave. She did the same and then walked out of his sight.

As she came closer to the village, she began to be nervous about what Jared and Anne might say. She was not the girl who had set out on a walk earlier that day. She knew that beyond any doubting, and so surely, she would seem different...look different. Her mind was full of what questions she might be asked when she arrived home and of what answers she would give. She hated lying, although there had been many times in the past when a lie had saved her from Anne's anger and Jared's fists, but this was not the same. She was so full of what had happened that she wanted them to know, wanted everyone to know, but the part of her that had sense and experience enough of her past life told her that this was something to be kept to herself. Perhaps there would be a time and place where she could speak but she knew that it was not now. Her first thought had been the only sensible thing to do. It was a secret. It was her secret.

In the event, all her fears proved groundless. When she came into the cottage, Anne was busy at the cooking pot and Jared was in the barn tending the horse. When later on they all sat at table together no questions were asked and as unbelievable as it seemed to Martha, it was as if it were just another mealtime, just another day, the same as all that had gone before it and all that would surely follow.

For Martha, the next few days passed as if in a dream. At night she lay in her bed and remembered what had happened, the words that had been spoken, the way Matthew had looked at her when he called out to her and she had turned, the feeling of his arms around her...and the kiss.

11
The Tree.

The following Sunday after church, during which she had sat through the service and the seemingly never-ending sermon by Henry Wilkin, she turned to Anne and Jared as they were all walking back through the churchyard and innocently asked if she could go for a walk.
"And don't you have any work to do at home?" Jared immediately answered.
Before she could reply, Anne said. "The work is all done, and beside which it is the Lord's day, so let her take a walk."
Jared moodily grunted his assent and so Martha left them at the churchyard gate and walked quickly down the lane that led out of the village not wanting to see anyone and perhaps be asked where she was going. She followed the path towards the river, all the while feeling a mixture of nervousness and anticipation. Would Matthew be there before her? what would they say and do?

After a while she came through the trees and into the small clearing that led down to the slope of the river bank and saw him. He had his back towards her and was facing the trunk of the tree where they had met before. As she came closer Matthew turned and she saw with a sudden shock that he was holding a knife. He must have realized that the sight of it had startled her and so he let it fall to the ground and opened his arms in welcome.
She moved into his embrace with a comfortable

ease as if they had already been together for years. For a few moments no words were spoken
 and then Matthew said "You came. I thought that perhaps..."
Martha interrupted him "Of course I came, did you not think that I would?"
Matthew smiled "No, what I meant was that I did not know if your brother would give you leave."
"If it had only been him he would not have done, but Anne agreed "
Matthew quickly bent down to pick up the knife which he sheathed into a leather holder on his belt. Martha looked past him to the tree trunk that he had been facing when she came along the path. She saw that there was an intricate design that had been carved into it. He turned and drew her closer to it.
"This is what I was doing when you came." His fingers traced the outline of the carving. "You see here is a letter M for my name and here entwined through and around it is another M for..."He looked to her for the answer.
"For Martha " she said softly
He nodded, "Yes, for Martha, and see, both are held within this design of a heart."
She moved forward and gently touched the outlines of his carving with her fingertips.
"It is beautiful."
Matthew smiled "And you are beautiful."
And then they kissed again, so naturally and with a sense of such ease that Martha knew that any thoughts she had felt in the last few days that this meeting might be somehow different and less than the time before were foolish. They both sat down

with their backs resting up against the old tree. They spoke of their lives. She told him of her birth and of the mother who had died. Matthew too had known and understood this loss as his own mother had died when he was but a child of five from a fever.

They talked of the world in which they lived and of the future and somehow, in a strange way and without anything specific being said, it seemed as if that future would be one in which they both were together.

……..

And so Sundays became their day, and the tree by the river became their place. Jared and Anne neither asked nor cared where Martha went on these afternoons as long as all her work was done. Martha did not really understand how it could have happened so quickly and completely. It was as if she understood everything and at the same time nothing. On the fourth Sunday that they met they walked down to the riverbank where they both stood hand in hand. There seemed to be an easy mutual silence between them. Although in the past few meetings they had talked of so many things it now somehow seemed as if no words were needed. Martha looked to where the water flowed and swirled, faster in some places and around the roots of the trees that were at the river's edge.

"I love you." Matthew said quietly.

Martha turned towards him. She had felt it...known it, and yet somehow now that the words had been spoken it was different. He looked at her, not knowing if she had heard above the sound of the river and repeated it.

"I love you."

He took both her hands. "Is it the same for you?"

She wanted to answer...to tell him, but all she could do was nod her head as he brought her closer into a tight embrace. He stroked her hair and said.

"I think I did love you the very first time I saw you at the market when you stood at my stall." he paused "Until I knew otherwise I feared that the man across the square was your man."

She smiled and shook her head. "Other than through birth, someone like that could never be a part of my life."

Martha rested within his arms. She was loved. Over and over the thought ran around her and through her. She was loved. Finally she felt herself able to speak.

"And I do love you Matthew."

There was no more to say, and never would be. Both knowing that, they kissed to seal the words and the moment forever.

Hand in hand they walked away from the river bank and back to the clearing.

"Will you be at the next market day?" he asked.

"I do not know if Jared will want to take me."

Matthew thought for a moment "Then ask to go with him, tell him it will be easier with your help."

"But even if he agrees and I'm there, we will not be able to meet."

"I want to speak with your brother, I want to tell him about us and perhaps try and make peace with him."

Martha looked down at the ground. "You don't

know him; he is not a man ever to make peace or forget what happened."

Matthew put his hand on her cheek and raised her head. "You may well be right but surely it is worth trying."

Martha thought back through all the years and said, "Jared is a hard and cruel man, there is no forgetting with him, nor any forgiveness in him."

"Martha, all this...all of what we are, has happened so quickly, but I feel it and I know it to be right, surely it would be better if he and I were at least not enemies."

"He has ever been my enemy." Martha replied sadly. "I can recall no moment of my life when he has shown me any kindness either in word or deed." she paused, "You have seen the marks on his face."

Matthew smiled "I would imagine that someone like him has been in many a fight and that he..."

"I did that to him." Martha said quietly.

Matthew made no answer and she continued "It was years ago...I had a bird that I had saved...a young raven. Jared was trying to hurt it and there was nothing I could do to stop him."

Matthew nodded "Yes, I can imagine him trying to harm a poor defenceless creature. I think you must have been a very brave child to have fought against him."

"I loved that bird. I had even given it a name. Beth...my mother's name."

"And did you save it?"

Martha smiled "Yes. It managed somehow to fly away though I never saw it again and it cost me the worst beating I ever had...but yes. I did save it."

Matthew was silent for a few moments. He took her face and held it gently between his hands.

"He will never...no-one will ever beat you again. There will be no man who can harm you, neither Jared or anyone else. I will be the man in your life. I will love you, care for you and protect you." he paused and looked into her eyes "As a good husband should."

The words that he had spoken seemed to hang suspended in the air between them. It was so right, so natural and Martha knew that no answer need be given. This was what life had held in store for her all those years. The hurts and sadness were all wiped clean. They mattered no more. There was a new life ahead for her...for them.

"And if we are to be wed" he continued "Then it would be right that..."

She knew what he was going to say and put a hand gently against his mouth to stop him. "There is no way that anything with Jared would ever be right." Martha paused and thought for a moment. "Could we not just leave without saying...without asking anything from anyone ?"

"Would that not look as if we were just running, that we were ashamed of our love." answered Matthew.

"Would that matter" she pleaded "Why would we need care what others thought or what they said of us. You have no family save for your uncle who you told me cares nothing for you and I have only Anne and Jared who I have no care for. We are nothing to our kinfolk other than cheap workers."

Matthew thought for a few moments and then nodded in agreement. "You are right but let us think how we can do it. If we wait for a couple of months, I can perhaps save a little from what my uncle gives me for the pottery I sell, and also it will give us some time to plan where we shall go and what we shall do."

"A couple of months seems like forever" Martha said feeling disappointed "I feel as if I want us to go right now."

"As I do, but it will only be a couple of months, and then it will be forever"

Martha thought about what Matthew had said and knew that he was right. She looked into his eyes. There was nothing else to say except to repeat his word.

"Forever."

They stood and embraced and with his arms tight around her, Martha could only in her happiness think of the word that she knew would help her to get through the weeks and months ahead.

Forever.

12
The Market.

And Martha did ask Jared if she could make the next trip to market with him and to her surprise, and for whatever reason of his own, he agreed.
The trip to Honiton was as it had been before but for Martha, as she sat beside a silent Jared as the cart traveled through the lanes and up and over the hills, she could feel the growing excitement at the thought of seeing Matthew. There was also a part of her that was fearful. Matthew had promised that there would be no trouble between him and Jared and that they would continue only to meet in their secret place until the time came for them to leave...but what if Jared saw him?

Finally they arrived in Honiton and went to their usual place where she dutifully helped Jared with as much as she could, tending to the horse and unloading his goods.
She shot a few quick glances across the wide market place and felt a huge sense of disappointment as she realized that Matthew was not there. He had said he was going to come but perhaps there had been a problem with his uncle, or possibly something had happened on the journey...a broken wheel or even...
And then suddenly she saw him. His stall was in a different position from the previous market day, a little further down the road. She saw that he was looking around and she hoped...no...she knew that he was looking for her.

He saw her and a huge smile came to his face. He raised an arm in greeting and she quickly looked towards Jared who was talking to one of the other traders. She hurriedly gave a wave in return and then turned away to continue helping setting up.

Throughout the morning she kept stealing glances towards Matthew's stall. He seemed to be doing good business and she was pleased for him knowing that the money would be a help to them as soon as they were ready to leave. She wondered whether she could risk going for a walk and possibly manage to have a few words with him without alerting Jared.

The day was hot and by the afternoon, trade had slackened and Martha began to hope that Jared might go off to the tavern. The thought would not leave her and finally she felt brave enough to suggest it. "It seems to be getting quiet now so if you want to go for some ale I could..." She stopped speaking as Jared looked directly at her with a quizzical expression on his face.

"I'll decide when I go for a drink...not you."

Martha quickly apologized. "I'm sorry Jared I just thought that..."

"Well don't think, and don't talk either."

The rest of the afternoon Martha stayed by the cart keeping her eyes down and not daring to look down the road towards Matthew's stall. Martha was almost relieved when it was time to start getting ready to pack up and prepare the cart for the journey back to Clanton. She knew that she would be able to meet with Matthew in their special place by the river on Sunday and so any conversation between them and plans that they would make would have to wait until then. She could not resist that one last look of the day and so quickly glanced towards Matthew's stall. He was looking towards her as if he was trying to make a decision. She felt a strange premonition that something was about to happen. The feeling lasted for a few heart stopping moments and then turned to certainty.

Martha felt a clutch of fear in her stomach as she watched Matthew slowly walk across the road towards them. Jared had been attending to the cart and turned to her angrily.
"Don't just stand there, help me with this and…"
He stopped as he saw Martha seemingly frozen to the spot and followed her gaze across the road, where seeing Matthew he suddenly tensed and began to clench his fists.
Matthew reached the cart and for a moment both men stood looking at each other.
"What do you want? "growled Jared
"I want nothing from you" answered Matthew, pausing for a moment "The last Market day…"
"I don't want to talk about that" replied Jared, his face becoming flushed.
"What's done is done and what's past is past. We're both working men and we both have to come to this market every month so surely it would be better if…"
"It would be better if you didn't come"
Martha watched as the two men faced up to each

other. She knew the signs and could see that Jared, whose face was becoming angrier by the moment was beginning to lose any control he might have had whilst Matthew was trying to keep the situation calmer. He turned his face away from Jared and glanced at Martha. The colour had drained from her face which was almost white with fear. When he looked back at Jared, he could see by a changed expression in his face that Jared had sensed something in the brief glance that had passed between them. He knew now that it had been foolish to try and make a peace with him, but he would make one last try. He slowly held out his open hand.

"If I am man enough to offer my hand, are you not man enough to take it."

Jared was silent for a moment. "I would not take it" he answered and then added contemptuously "I would not ever spit on it."

Matthew made no reply. He turned and slowly walked back across the road.

Martha watched him go trying not to look at Jared but sensing that he was staring at her and becoming painfully aware that her face was beginning to blush.

Jared did not speak until they had left the market well behind them and were on their way home."
"You know him, don't you?"

Martha felt herself reddening. She hated the fact that she could not just speak the truth and be done with it. "I know that he comes to the market and sells his pots and that..."

Jared interrupted her angrily "Don't lie to me you little bitch. I saw a look that you gave each other. That's why you wanted me to go off for a drink. That's what you do when you go for your walks. Are you his whore...do you let him have you?"
Martha's mind was spinning. She didn't know what to say, how to explain. She was stung and bewildered by Jared's accusation. There was no more time or chance for secrecy now. She had to explain.
"Jared you do not understand. It is not like that. We have planned to speak to you and Anne."
"Oh you have planned have you" he sneered. "Do you think you'll just go off together. What about all the work you need to do in the house. We've kept you for all these years. Do you think that was out of love ?"
Martha felt a sudden rush of anger. "I know it was never for love, and is that all I am to you and Anne....a servant?"
Jared looked at her with a look of contempt. "You are less than that to me."
Martha had a sudden urge to just jump out of the cart and run back towards Honiton in the hope that Matthew might still be there, but she knew that was impossible as they had already been on the road for nearly an hour. She wanted nothing more now than to get back to Clanton and for the day to be done with.
The remainder of the journey continued in silence until they had come back into the village and driven the cart into the barn, Jared finally spoke.
"You say nothing of this to Anne."

Martha protested " Jared, can we not now all speak of it and I can tell you about..."

"I don't want to speak of it. I don't want to hear of it. Do you understand?"

"Martha felt herself becoming tearful with frustration. "But if only..."

She stopped as Jared clenched his hand into a fist and held it threateningly above her face as if about to strike.

"Do you understand me you bitch?"

Martha slowly nodded, got down from the cart and started to unhitch the horse as Jared turned and walked out of the barn and towards the cottage.

13
Jared

He couldn't sleep. He lay awake next to Anne listening to her snoring and kept wondering about Martha and Matthew. Had they been lovers? He knew she'd denied it and part of him believed her. He thought about Martha. That long black hair, the pale face, her breasts. How could Matthew not have taken her. He thought about his own life with Anne. Perhaps if he hadn't been scarred by the bitch then he might have had more choices with some of the other young women of the village. It wasn't only the look of Anne; she was becoming ever more bitter about their lack of children as if that was his fault when any fool knew that it was the woman's duty to conceive.

He thought again about Martha and the few secret glimpses he'd had of her when she was getting dressed and she'd not known that he was spying on her. He felt himself hardening as he imagined her totally naked. He thought of all the things he would like to do to her, and what made it worse was the fact that she was there, only a few feet away in a small side room at the other end of the cottage. If only Anne were not there. But she was there, and he turned towards her and began to lift her night shift. He ran his hand over her thighs and then up towards her breasts. He touched her nipples and she drowsily moved towards him. He moved on top and eased himself into her. She was still half asleep and became more awake as closing his eyes and imagining it was Martha's yielding body beneath him, he began to thrust more savagely.

This was how he imagined it would be. Martha would take him; it was what she owed for what she had done to his face. Anne was awake now and moving in time with him. He started to move towards a climax. Yes...even if it was only to be this once, he was grasping and enjoying every moment that Martha was giving him. He was almost there. He knew that she was as aroused as he was. Her fingers were digging into his back...it was coming...he heard her cry out beneath him "Jared..." He couldn't hold back anymore; he finished and spoke her name...

"Martha "

At the same moment that he felt the release of his passion he felt the body beneath him grow rigid. He opened his eyes and saw those of Anne glaring at him first in an uncomprehending disbelief and then with fury. He tried to think of something to say, a way to explain, but even as his mind was crowding with excuses Anne was clawing at his face. He pulled away from her and tried to cover his face with his hands but she still came at him, and now she also started to shout.

"You bastard, you filthy bastard?"

As he jumped out of the bed to try and escape Anne's fury and her wild blows, he heard a sound behind him and turned to see Martha standing there her eyes wide with uncomprehending fear of the scene in front of her.

Anne had also got out of the bed and for a few moments there was silence as she looked first at

Jared and then at Martha.

There was a dead silence for a few moments and then Anne rushed at Martha and slapped her hard across the face making her stagger backwards. Anne turned again towards Jared who was standing with his back to the wall. Her voice was cold and hard "Is that who you think of when you do it to me?"

"It's not. I mean I..."Jared stuttered

"I care not what you mean...you'll not touch me again" she looked away from him and at Martha. "Do you two. Have you ever...?"

For a brief moment Martha did not understand what Anne meant and then with a sickening feeling that flooded through her…she did. "Oh Anne. How could you ever think...? I wanted to tell you" said Martha, still shocked by what had happened. "There is someone that wants to be with me...wants to marry me. His name is Matthew and it was Jared who said I should not speak of it."

Anne spat out the words "He can have you. Anyone can have you for what I care of it. Now get back to your bed and out of my sight."

Still not even beginning to understand what had happened, and with her face reddened and stinging from Anne's blow, Martha did as she was told without looking at either Anne or Jared.

She lay awake trying to understand what had taken place. She could not sleep and as the hours passed, the silence of the rest of the night seemed louder than any words could have been. Whatever had happened... whatever the reasons...it did not matter anymore. Anne and Jared had their own life and now she knew that she was to have hers. She had told them about Matthew and their plans. From now on there was no need for it to be a secret.

14
The Truth.

Somehow a couple of hours of restless sleep must have finally come as she awoke to the sound of Anne opening the door of her room. Anne looked towards her and saw that she was awake.
"Get up and dressed there's work to be done." she said sharply.
Martha got out of bed. "Is Jared..."
Anne didn't wait for her to finish. "Jared left early this morning, he be staying with Ralph, or some other of his useless friends."
Martha quickly dressed and going to the basin and jug in the corner, splashed some cold water on her face before starting on her usual chores.
Anne remained silent and grim faced as she went about her own work, and for her part Martha knew better than to even try and talk to her.
As the morning passed Anne's attitude and behavior slowly seemed to change and Martha noticed that any looks Anne did give her were less hostile.

By mid-day and with the morning's work finished, Anne looked at Martha. "Come and sit " she said softly, pointing to a stool. Martha did as she was asked wondering what was about to be said. Anne sat opposite her and closed her eyes for a moment.
"I'm sorry" she said quietly.
Martha was surprised by the change in Anne's voice. "Last night..." she nervously began "I do not understand what happened. What it was all about?" she said.

The previous night's anger seemed to have drained away, Anne half smiled sadly "And my wish for you is that you never come to know of things like this. My hope for you and your Matthew is that your life together does not hold the things that are between your brother and me."

Martha had never known Anne to take this tone of voice with her. It was as if Anne had realized something new and different about her and that she was being spoken to as an equal and as one woman to another. For the moment she didn't know how to respond, what to say or how much to say. " Anne, I don't want to..."she began.

Anne interrupted her with a slow shake of her head. "Martha, there is no need to say anything. Now, tell me of this boy, what does he do? where does he live?"

It was as if a flood had been released in Martha and she was able to tell of all that she had been holding inside her, and so she told Anne of how and where she and Matthew had met, though she remembered to leave out the fight he had had with Jared on that first market day. She told of his trade, of his kindness and care for her and of the plans they had made, to go away, possibly to Exeter and make a new life for themselves.

Anne's face and expression had softened as she spoke, and Martha felt encouraged to speak of their hopes for the future and for the life together that she and Matthew might have.

Finally Martha felt she had said all that could be told and was silent.

"And when would you be going?" asked Anne quietly.

"Perhaps in a month or two" replied Martha "Matthew says that he owes his uncle the time to find and take on an apprentice or someone to take over his work." She paused before adding "And also to see if it will be all right with both you and Jared."

Anne gave her a long look before answering. "It is right that you should go and find you own life, and as for Jared, whatever he says or thinks, it will be as I say, so whenever you next meet your Matthew you may tell him of what I have said".

Though still shaken from the events of the previous night, Martha felt relieved at what Anne was saying. Now she and Matthew could make their plans in the open and after all, she thought, what was a month or two set against a future lifetime.

A day later Jared returned. He seemed subdued and tried to keep himself to himself. There was little if any talk between him and Anne, and the atmosphere in the cottage, which in all Martha's memory had never been good, now seemed even worse with the air full of unspoken hostility.

For her part, Anne's attitude towards Martha seemed changed since their talk and it was almost as if a new silent agreement and understanding existed between them.

…......................................

Three days later in the early morning, what had become the usual cold silence in the cottage was broken by a sound outside followed by a loud knocking at the door. Jared looked at Anne and then slowly began to rise from the chair where he had been pulling on his boots. The knocking became more insistent. "All right, I'm coming" he shouted as he reached and opened the door. It was Anne's uncle William who rushed past Jared and into the room. "Anne…it's your father. There's been a bad accident."

Anne stopped what she'd been doing and looked at him "What...is he?"

William shook his head and then breathlessly explained how Anne's father had been kicked in the head by a horse he was trying to shoe and had been unconscious since the previous evening.

"Is he like to die?" asked Anne anxiously.

"I don't be knowin' but it might be good if you were by him."

Martha had never heard Anne speak much about her family but could see that the news had shaken her as she immediately started to bustle about gathering some things together.

"How long might you be?" asked Martha.

Anne gave her a scornful look. "And how would I know that you fool. It will be as long as it need to be."

"I'm sorry" said Martha, stung by Anne's response. For his part Jared had said nothing and had just continued standing by the table.

"I'll come with you " offered Martha. "I can be of help. There might be some herbs or healing I could use that might..."

"And who's to do the work here" Anne replied angrily looking at Jared. "For certain not him. I'll not come back to a filthy mess."

Martha knew there was no sense in arguing so just went to the corner of the cottage for a broom to begin her usual morning housework.

Within a few minutes Anne had thrown a few things into a bag and was ready to leave.

"I hope that your father will be well." said Martha.

"He'll be as God wants him to be" answered Anne as she and her uncle walked out of the door.

As she stood just outside the doorway and watched Anne and her uncle drive away in his small cart, Martha felt a strange chill run through her despite the warmth of the June day. She turned back into the cottage to continue her own work before she would be able to do Anne's.

At the door, Jared roughly pushed past her. "I'm going to the barn to see to the horse and then I be goin' to see Ralph."

Martha felt relief at the prospect of time on her own and quietly asked him "When will you be back?"

He suddenly spun round and grabbed her by the throat. "I don't answer to you. I be back whenever I wants to and all you need to do is be sure to have a meal ready for me."

The shock of his action and the anger in his voice stunned her. She felt herself choking and was terrified of what he was going to do. Then, just as quickly as he had grabbed her, he released his grip and walked out of the cottage and towards the barn.

15
Before.

The day had passed slowly. She'd finished all of the housework, both hers and Anne's, and prepared an evening stew for whenever Jared would return, and now she sat by the fire where the cauldron had been heating for a couple of hours. She had fears of it being ruined and then having to face Jared's anger but though it was dark now she knew she could neither eat her own meal before she had served her brother nor go to her bed and leave the fire unattended. The light of the fire and a single candle between them seemed to throw flickering and twisted patterns against the rough walls of the room.

Suddenly she heard a noise outside. There was laughter and shouting and she realized it was the sound of Jared and his friends and that they had been drinking. Of course she should have known that once Anne was away then he would spend his time in the tavern. Well, she thought, better that than it would have been for him to stay home and sit morosely by the fire looking at her in that strange way that he had been doing since she had told him about Matthew, and all the more so whenever Anne was not in the room.

The sounds outside quieted as Jared's friends, Edward, Ralph and Thomas went off their separate ways and then the door opened, and Jared staggered into the room immediately falling over and cursing. Even from a few feet away she could smell not just the ale but also the stink of vomit on him. She stood up and moved towards him to help him up, feeling a sickness come to her as she reached out an arm to assist him. He angrily knocked it away and slowly got to his feet.

"There is food for you brother, it may help you to feel better."

Even after a lifetime of Jared's hardness and cruelty, the look he gave her made her fear him as she had never done before.

"It is not food I want." he said slowly, his eyes going from her face down her body and back again to her face where he saw a look of horror as she understood his meaning.

There were no words she felt able to speak other than his name.

"Jared."

"What be the matter…am I not good enough for you? Are you saving yourself for your Matthew" he smiled, "Or has he already tasted your delights…is that it?"

Martha was stunned by what he was suggesting and by the tone of his voice.

"Jared…brother. I swear to you before God that I am still a maid. I have not known any man."

A long silence as they both stood there, held within the moment. Martha knew there was nothing she could say but tried to speak to him through the fear and pleading in her eyes. It seemed as if a spell surrounded them that stopped time itself. She looked into his eyes, into his face, where he now moved his hand and touched the scarred and puckered skin at the right side.

"Then Martha…sister, it is surely time that you did."

He moved towards her as she quickly tried to reach for the ladle that was on the hearth by the side of the pot. Despite his drunkenness he was quicker and kicked it away and out of reach.

"That will never happen again " he shouted as at the same time he brought the back of his hand across her face, knocking her to the floor. She lay there hoping that the blow might have lessened and used his anger. He looked down at her and his hands reached down to untie his britches.

She tried to stand up but, in a moment he was down upon her grabbing at her thin dress, lifting it up and then roughly forcing her legs apart.

Through her terror she tried to think clearly and reason with him "Jared. For the love of God, you know this is a sin, you know it is wrong."

There was no answer as he pulled down his britches and then roughly pushed and entered her. She gave a cry as the sudden pain swept through her body and brought her hands up to claw at his face. In response he knocked them away and clenching his fist gave her a savage blow to the cheek.

The force of the punch would have rendered her unconscious had she not been able to turn her head at the last moment, though she wished that it might have done to spare her from the tearing pain down below as Jared continued to thrust and pound on top of her. She prayed that the hurting and the nightmare of what he was doing to her would end. In her mind she called out to a God that she now knew either was not listening or did not care.

And then suddenly what had been Jared's drunken grunting gave way to a long groan and then a final triumphant shout and it was over. He lay panting for a few more moments and then pulled out of her, rolling to the side and then staggering to his feet. Martha remained where she lay on the floor feeling herself torn and broken from a wound she knew would never heal.

…...

The next morning she slowly opened her eyes to the new day and immediately felt a burning pain between her legs. Her mind was overwhelmed by the memory of what had been done to her the night before, and she realized that she was still laying on the floor where Jared had left her.

She pulled her dress down to cover her nakedness and turned slowly onto her side facing the wall, at the same time listening to hear if Jared was still near.

He was, and now that he knew she was awake he shouted at her.

"Get up"

She slowly and painfully rose to her feet and started to back away from where Jared was standing in the doorway with an angry scowl on his face.

There were a few moments of silence and then he moved towards her. She was gripped by a fear that it was all about to happen again and pressed herself into the corner against the wall. Jared moved closer and roughly grabbed hold of her neck. There was a moment of paralysing fear that he was about to kill her to protect himself after what had happened. She could feel his stinking breath as he brought his face to within a few inches of hers.

"You listen to me. If you speak a word of what happened to Anne, or to anyone…I'll kill you."

Martha looked into his face and made no answer.

"Do you understand what I say…do you believe me?"

Martha tried to form the words, but her mouth was dry with fear, instead she just nodded her head. Jared moved his hand towards her face, and she flinched as he fingered the bruise that had formed from his punch as she had tried to fight him off and protect herself.

"And if you're asked about this then you just say that you fell."

He moved his hand from her face and grabbed at her hair pulling her head backwards "What do you say?"

Martha whispered the answer he wanted. "I say that I fell."

And Anne did ask. When she had returned from her father's house later that day where she had been of no more use than to sit by his side and watch him die, and though everything in Martha wanted to tell what had happened and to seek some comfort, she also knew that a threat from Jared was very real. It would be better to keep silent and to try to learn to live with the secret and the shame. Anne now had her own grief to nurse. There were moments when Martha wondered if perhaps one day the memory would fade and dim as the pain of her body and the bruise on her face would slowly but surely heal. She knew it would not.

16
After.

They sat against the trunk of what they now called their tree and looked down the bank and towards the river. It had been a strange meeting. Five days had passed and although the bruise on her face was almost gone, of course Matthew had noticed it. She had told him the same lie that she had told Anne, that she had fallen and caught her face against a table. He had looked at her quizzically, feeling that there was more to tell but sensing that this was perhaps not the time and that Martha would speak when and if she wanted or was able to. For her part Martha felt that what had happened, what Jared had done to her must surely be written into her face. She felt that she must look different or sound different and that the feelings and emotions that had filled her since that dreadful night must have some outward showing.

She had been terrified when Anne had returned to her own village for her father's funeral two days later, but Jared had been out in the day and by the time he came back in the evening Anne had returned.
She tried to think only of the future and although she felt happy and positive as they continued to make their plans, she was also painfully aware of the hurt and damage that seemed to be locked inside her. She forced herself to smile as Matthew told of the arrangements that would soon become reality and hoped that he would not see the pain that she

felt inside, reflected in her eyes.
The weeks passed and Martha waited and longed only for the times when she could meet with Matthew. When they were together it was as if she were a different person. The life that lay ahead of them seemed so real that she almost forgot the secret hurt she carried. She felt that Matthew's love and gentleness would somehow wipe it away in the years that were to come.
It was only when they parted, and she began to walk back towards the cottage that her inner sadness grew with every step.

Within the cottage, life and the daily routine continued as if nothing had happened or changed. Sometimes she was aware of Jared slyly looking at her, though she tried never to meet his eyes. Even when Anne was outside, or they were alone together Jared acted as he always had done towards her. She even sometimes wondered if perhaps he was ashamed of what he'd done and of the sin he had committed.
There were times, laying in her bed at night when the welcome forgetfulness of sleep was just about to come and her whole being seemed overwhelmed by the memory of what had happened, and she was suddenly wide awake and reliving every moment. It was if she could feel Jared's rough hands clawing at her and could smell his drunken breath.
On nights like these she would try to think of other things... better things.
In the past she had known the happiness that Beth had brought her though those days, like the bird

itself were long gone. In the future there was only Matthew. She tried to imagine the life they would have and wondered whether there would ever come a time when she could either forget what had happened or if not that then at least be able to look back on it as one remembers an accident from long ago where the pain and scars have healed.

17.
Telling

August 1608.

There was no one she could ask. No one she could speak to, and yet she knew. She knew it as much in her mind as in her body. That first month when her flow had not come, she had thought, had perhaps hoped, that the shock of what had happened to her, what Jared had done to her, might have affected her rhythms. When the second month came and passed it brought only certainty.
The thought was with her during all the day but was worse when she lay in her bed at night. Her mind was spinning with the thoughts of what she could do. Could she run away? But how and where to. Could she tell Anne? Of course not, she knew what the very first question would be. Could she tell Matthew...she felt sick at the very thought.

And what of Matthew and their plans, their life together. She realized bitterly that it was never to be. She had been so foolish to think that after all her early years, then suddenly a new good life would be hers. What right had she to have expected such a thing. No there was in truth only one person who could be told, who should be told.

He was in the barn clearing out the cart and took no notice of her as she came in.
"Jared."
He answered without even looking round." What do

you want"

"I must talk with you." she said quietly.

"If it be about your plans then I don't care what you and your damned potter boy do, you can both go to hell for all that it matter to me."

Martha felt a sudden anger come over her and raised her voice in a way she had never dared to use with Jared before. "Look at me."

Jared stopped what he had been doing and slowly turned to face her, as much surprised at the way she had spoken as Martha had been herself.

There was a moment of stilled silence before she spoke.

"I am with child."

Jared looked as stunned as if he had been struck. "How do you know that? Have you spoken with anyone?" A look of sudden panic came over his face. "Does Anne..."

"No, but I have not had my flow for two months now and I know that…"

"What's that to me" he interrupted "It will be from your precious Matthew…you go and tell him."

"It cannot be him. You know well that I've not lain with him, nor anyone else. The only time was when...when you took me"

He made a sudden move towards Martha and grabbed her arm "Shut your mouth…if you speak those words again they will be your last."

"But what am I to do? What can I tell Matthew?"

Jared gave her a sly grin. "You tell him nothing. You can be wed in a matter of weeks. You will open your legs for him on your wedding night, or sooner if you have any sense, and he can claim the child"

Martha was shocked "I cannot do that to him, it would not be right."

He increased the pressure on her arm so she cried out

"Listen to me you stupid bitch, you don't have any choice. If you breathe even a word to Anne or anyone. I'll kill you, so that be the only thing you do have to choose, life or death."

Martha made no reply. It was Jared who spoke again

"Life or death Martha. For you... and for the baby."

She looked into his face which was now twisted with rage and hate and she knew that he spoke the truth, and even if she would choose death for herself which she knew to be a mortal sin, how much worse a sin if she were to destroy the life that was growing inside her.

He pulled her closer to him and she felt his stinking breath as he spat out the words "You choose....and choose now."

She felt such a fear that any words she would speak did not... could not come. Jared dragged her over to the side of the barn where there were tools laying on a bench. He picked up an iron bar and held it above her face " One last time I ask you...choose."

She somehow found the strength to overcome the fear "Life. I choose life. I swear I'll not speak of what you did."

Jared looked into her eyes and for a terrifying moment she thought that he would not take the risk of believing or trusting her. Then he released his grip on her. She fell backwards to the ground. He looked down at her. "If you have any sense, you and your potter should leave now and be done with it." He turned away and walked back to the cart, though still holding the iron bar. Slowly Martha got to her feet. She did not know what she had expected Jared to say or do when she told him, she was so frightened and confused herself that she'd not thought beyond that moment.

She left the barn and walked back to the cottage. Thankfully Anne had gone out so at least she had the chance to be on her own for a while. She couldn't think of what to do next. Could she tell Matthew the truth of it and would he believe her, would anyone believe her?

She knew that her life as she'd thought it might be was over. Her hopes and dreams. Over. But this other life, this life inside her.

...It was beginning.

18
And Telling.

August 1608.

It was their own special place, and had been ever since he had carved their initials and love heart into the bark of the old tree by the river bank and until today it had always been a place of joy and of love, but today…today surely that would change. As usual Matthew was there before her. She saw him from a little way away and stopped. He was sitting and leaning with his back against the tree looking at the river as it flowed. Whatever was to happen next, she wanted to fix this one moment inside of her. She felt any courage she might have had just drain from her. She suddenly knew that there was no way she would be able to speak the words that she had prepared. There really was only one thing left to do. She knew that this moment now would have to be the last time she ever saw him. One final look before she turned away…
"Martha "
He had looked up and seen her and was getting to his feet.
She turned and began to run back the way she had come. She had not gone more than a few steps before Matthew had caught up with her.
"Martha, what is wrong? Why are you crying? "
Her voice, when she was able to speak was choked.
"It cannot be. We cannot be."
Matthew looked stunned and disbelieving. "What are you saying? Do you no longer love me?

Why…how could you change so?"

"Oh Matthew, it is not me. It could never be me."

"What then. It's almost time for us to leave...just a week or so"

She knew then that she must tell him. No matter what happened he must never leave her now thinking that her love had changed.

"It is Jared…he"

Matthew looked uncomprehending. "What has Jared to do with this, has he now forbidden our match?"

"Not forbidden, he wants us to be wed as soon as possible."

"So what then could be wrong?"

There was that one single moment when a voice inside her thought on what Jared had told her…to open her legs, wed without delay and then swear the child was Matthew's. Other girls had done no less. Other girls had learned to live with such a secret. There would be other children and they would surely be Matthew's.

He stood in front of her, his face full of worry and concern, but even so, his eyes were full of love and she knew that the life she had wanted with him, the life she had hoped for, could not be lived with a lie. She closed her eyes rather than meet his as she spoke the words. "Matthew. I am with child."

Nothing. Not a word. Not a sound. She forced herself to open her eyes and saw such a pain in his face that she knew she had to tell it all before any courage she might have had deserted her. " There's worse to tell. " she paused and took a deep breath "Two months since, when Anne had gone away to her father's deathbed, Jared...Jared took me by force. You remember when we met, and my face was bruised, and I told you I had fallen."

Matthew closed his eyes for a moment his face creased with pain. "I had a feeling, somehow you were different that day when you told me, but at worst I thought that he might have hit you and that you did not want me to know."

Martha closed her eyes and continued "I was so scared of what you might have wanted to do, that was why I kept silent about...about." Suddenly Martha could hold back no more and began to weep.

Matthew's face had now taken on an expression that she had never seen before, an expression that she had not thought him capable of. It was pure angry hatred. He spat out the words "I'll kill him for what he's done. I'll come back to Clanton now and face him and…."

Martha seized his hands and held them tightly "No. He said that if I told anyone that it was him then he would kill me, and I know...you know that he could do it."

There were a few moments of silence, neither of them knowing what to say.

Though she felt that her heart was breaking and that this might well be their last time together, Martha also felt relieved that she'd found the courage to be honest with him and to be true to herself.

She could see Matthew trying to make sense of it all and thinking of what they could now do. Finally he spoke, his voice firm and the decision made. "We shall go away. It will be all right. We can make a life for ourselves and no one will know of what was done to you. The child will be ours. I can find work and we can…" he stopped as the strength in Martha gave way and all the emotion she had been trying to hold within herself since she had realized about the baby broke down and made way for an uncontrolled sobbing. Matthew took her head between his hands and kissed her tears. "I promise you; it will be better. This time will surely pass and will come to seem as just a bad memory, a wound, an injury from which you shall…we shall recover."

Martha looked into his eyes and felt herself filled with the strength of his certainty. She felt herself blessed to have a love like this.

"When shall we go ?" she whispered.

"As soon as we can. There is nothing to stay here for. Go back now and gather what you can carry for the journey. I will go back and do the same. It is too late now to travel but if we can set out early in the morning we could make towards Exeter " A sudden look of concern came over Matthew's face "Will you be safe... will Jared..."

"Do not fear, Anne is there and even if he were to know I was leaving he would care none, it's what he wants."

"Well do not take any chances or say anything that will anger him."

Martha reached up and caressed the side of Matthew's face.

"I will say nothing. I will do nothing, except think of the new life that begins for us tomorrow."

Matthew smiled "Go now my sweet love, but one

kiss before we meet again."
He drew her into his arms holding her tightly. Their lips touched and held together. Martha felt as if the pain and worry that had consumed her was somehow slipping away and being replaced by the warmth of the knowledge that as long as Matthew was by her side nothing could cause her unhappiness again. For his part Matthew felt a loving protectiveness for this girl who he knew was to be the love of his life. He wished only that the coming hours would fly away and that they would be here in this place again tomorrow on the start of their journey.
And each knew that the decision was right and that a fresh beginning awaited them.

19
The River.

Matthew watched till Martha was out of sight and then turned back towards his own village. His mind was racing with all that had happened and of the practicalities of the journey they would start the next day. First they would make for Honiton and meet the city road that would take them to Exeter. Perhaps they might gain a lift from a carter traveling that way. Once there they would need to find somewhere cheap to lodge. He stopped and listened, feeling sure that he had heard voices. Nothing…just the natural sounds of the woods. He continued down the path and stopped again. He had an uneasy sense that something was not right. His thoughts went to Martha. He should have walked with her back to Clanton, at least to the outskirts of the village, perhaps if he turned around now he would catch up with her and see that she was safe.
 He made the decision and started back along the path he had just come down. A few steps and then he stopped again, this time certain that he was not alone. He looked around but could see nothing. He was overcome by the knowledge that he had been wrong not to go back with Martha. He began to move off again but had only gone a few paces when he stopped and stared in stunned disbelief as a few feet away he saw that Jared had stepped out from behind a tree.
He was filled with a sudden and overwhelming anger. "You" he shouted, readying himself for the fight he knew was coming.

"Yes…me" answered Jared with a sneer "What are you going to do about it"

Matthew moved towards Jared, his fists beginning to clench, "I'm going to make you pay for what you did to Martha…I'm going to drag you back to the village and force you to own to your crime and sin. I'll not have them all think bad of her"

The self-satisfied and confident look remained on Jared's face as he replied "They do know her for what she is" he pointed to the scarring that ran down the side of his face "They have known for years, since she did this to me."

"I know why that happened…Martha told me and she …"

He stopped speaking as he saw another man step out and stand beside Jared.

Matthew looked from one to the other. "So you are a coward as well as being an animal who would rape his own sister."

Jared gave a mocking laugh. "Did she tell you it was rape? Yes I suppose that is what she would have said…oh no you fool…it was done with her being all too willing."

Matthew felt the rage boil up inside him…no matter that there were two of them. He made to move forward but suddenly and with shock found himself grabbed and held on either side from behind. His arms were pulled back and he felt a rope binding his hands together. He struggled desperately but was knocked to the ground by a blow to the back of his head. He tried to stand up but as he did so Jared rushed towards him and punched him in the stomach. Matthew felt a sudden rush of bile in his mouth as he fell to his knees. The men holding him from behind brought him to his feet to where Jared and his companion faced him.

"You are not so ready to deal with me now are you."

"If I were not held you would see what I would do" replied Matthew.

In response Jared slowly brought his hand up in front of Matthew's face and made a show of slowly clenching it, "This one is for what happened at Honiton market." he smirked, before just as slowly drawing it back and then with as much force as he could summon, punching Matthew straight in the face.

There was a sickening crunch as the blow broke his nose and Matthew felt spouts of warm blood flowing down his face.

He felt his knees buckle and would have fallen were he not held securely by the two men who had grabbed him from behind.

"What do you say now of what you would do" taunted Jared.

"Against you alone…I still know what I would do "gasped Matthew ,"But against four I can only know you for the coward you are."

Jared brought his face closer. "A coward am I...Well this coward is going to teach you that you should never have crossed me."

He had been in fights before but had never received a beating such as this. His mind was overcome by the shame of what was being done to him without his being able to fight back and his body felt more damaged with each blow that landed. It seemed never ending but finally Jared dealt him a savage punch into the stomach, and he felt himself sinking down as the men that had held him released their grip. He lay on the ground as the four men stood over him. The beating had stopped and through a haze of pain Matthew wondered if they had decided that he could take no more and were going to just leave him out here. Somehow, he would have to drag himself back to his village... there would be help there and he could have some time to recover. His mind was in a daze…there was no time…he was to meet Martha the following morning and they were to …"

His thoughts were stopped as Jared slammed his foot into Matthew's ribs and laughed. "Look at you now. Not so proud are you…I don't even think my whore of a sister would want you."

The other men laughed as Jared continued "I think perhaps we need to clean away all that blood." Matthew was grabbed by the arms and roughly pulled to his feet. Every movement sent waves of agonizing pain through his body as he tried to assess what damage had been done to him but at the same time he felt himself sinking into a welcoming unconsciousness as he was dragged back along the path towards the clearing by the river where in what now seemed a lifetime ago he had stood with Martha.

There was now a silence among the men that was somehow far worse and more threatening than their shouts and taunts when they had been beating him and through the pain now came a different fear. They reached the water's edge and paused for a few moments as if in either final hesitation or decision and then without any further words being spoken Matthew was pulled down the slope of the bank and into the river. Though the savage beating had left him almost semi-conscious the sudden iciness of the water took his breath away as they dragged him in and out towards where the fast-flowing water came up to their knees. They were all around him as if each of them wanted to share in what Matthew now knew was to be the last few moments of his life. He felt his head grasped by the hair and forced down beneath the surface where the shock of the water brought him back to an awareness of what was happening.

His head was beneath the water now as he desperately tried to hold on to the last breath left in his body…to prolong even the pain and fear because it was still life. There was a sensation of falling into blackness. He wanted to call out her name one last time before he surrendered but knew it was beyond him, so he thought and named it in his ever-fading mind. "Martha…Martha."
Then suddenly he was pulled up above the water's surface where he hungrily gulped in as much of the air as he could. There was a momentary wave of desperate hope, perhaps this was to be it…a beating and being half drowned. It was to have been a lesson…a warning. He looked up into Jared's face grimacing now into a strange exultant expression that was both satisfaction and hate and knew that he

was wrong. One last deep breath and this time he was able to shout it out…towards wherever she was.

"Martha…"

It was over in a few moments. Jared forced Matthew's head down into the water again whilst the others held the struggling and twisting body that soon became still.

There were a few moments of silence as Edward, Ralph, Thomas and Jared looked to each other. It was Thomas who spoke "What do we do with him now?"

"We just leave him; he'll float down river and away from here." answered Jared.

"Are you mad" said Ralph. "He'll be found and questions will be asked."

"We'll bury him in the woods" said Jared. "That way it will look as if he just went missing or ran off."

They all considered this and then Ralph asked, "And why would he run off ?"

This time it was Edward who spoke "What do that matter. He's not from our village...no one knows, no one cares, it be the best thing to do"

No one said anything more and in silent agreement they dragged the battered and lifeless body back to the bank. It only took a few minutes more to find a place not far from the ancient tree in the clearing where the ground dipped down into a hollow and using only their knives and hands had scooped out a shallow grave into which they threw Matthew's body covering it over with some fallen branches and bracken. And then they walked away.

20
Searching

Though it was only late August somehow there was the smell of autumn in the early morning air. A few leaves were already browning and would soon be falling.
She had left the cottage at first light leaving everything behind, her only thought to be as quiet as possible so as not to wake Anne or Jared.
Martha felt a growing excitement as she neared their meeting place. The night had felt so strange. It had seemed that the time was passing so slowly and, in another way, that it was rushing by. She had drifted in and out of a troubled sleep wanting only to be up and to have left the cottage before anyone was awake. Jared had come home late that night and had looked at her in a strange way as if somehow, he knew of her plans or if not that then of something else. No matter, the night was over, the time had come and, in a few minutes, they would be together again.

She knew Matthew loved her, but she had not realized how much until those moments the day before when she had told him about the baby, and now that knowledge somehow warmed and calmed her as she hurried towards where Matthew would be waiting. They would go away to where they were not known. They would put the past and Jared behind them. A new life. A new beginning.
She arrived at the clearing half expecting to see Matthew there before her. No matter. She knew it

would only be a matter of minutes before he came, and what was that compared to the lifetime that stretched ahead of them. She sat down on the grass with her back leaning against the tree. She felt so many emotions as she waited. There was excitement and there was hope. There was also fear at what the future might hold for them both, but she knew that with Matthew by her side she would find the strength to face anything.

The time passed and she began to have a feeling of unease. Had she arrived too early? She would wait. She knew that these were only the final moments of her having to be alone. Soon he would be here and their journey...their life together would start.
More time passed and although she tried her best to be patient, somehow the unease was slowly turning to fear. Why had Matthew not come? Perhaps he had been delayed and would be here soon, although she suddenly thought, he had always been the first to arrive at their special place. As the time went on there were even moments when she began to doubt and then hated herself for that doubt. Knowing that she had to do something…anything rather than just wait; she began to walk towards Matthew's village which she knew to be about four miles away.

Each step and with each small passage of time she looked ahead in expectation of seeing him running towards her. He would be breathless and full of apologies. There would be reasons…explanations. She played it through in her mind. They would laugh about it as they set of to…to where…it did not matter; they would be together.

Just under three hours later she came over the last hill and saw the village below with trails of smoke from the hearths and fires rising into the air. She walked down into the winding street suddenly thinking that she did not know where Matthew lived or even what his uncle was called. As she came to the first few houses, she saw an old man carrying a bundle of kindling on his shoulder. She walked over to him and quietly asked if he knew where Matthew lived, at the same time realizing that she knew him by no other name. The man stopped, listened and looked at her as if he could not even understand her question, so she asked it of him again, and again the same blank response. As she stood there a girl of about her own age came over to them.

"There's a wasting of your time to be talking to old Simon, he's had the deafness on him for years."

The old man looked at them both and then giving a shrug and a toothless grin slowly walked off.

Martha turned to her "Then can you tell me if you know of Matthew?"

"And which Matthew would that be?" the girl answered. "There's Matthew who is the son of the blacksmith or there be Matthew the potter's kin."

"Yes that's the one. The potter is his uncle, that is who I mean." Martha answered quickly.

"Well he do live at the other end of the village."

Martha felt her hopes rise as the girl pointed the way and then her whole-body freeze as the girl continued.

"Old Walter has been out searching for him since he had not been seen since yester' mornin.'"

Martha felt stunned by the answer. There were more questions rushing through her mind than she could put into words. A woman had noticed the girls talking and had come over to where they stood. She had a hard and angry face and looked at Martha and the other girl as if they had no right to even be talking.

"What be the matter"

The girl turned towards the woman.

"She be asking after Matthew…him that's gone missin'."

The woman took a long look at Martha.

"And why should you be asking after him?"

Martha did not know how to reply. Though she had never met this woman she could feel the lack of any kindness or sympathy.

"Well…he is…"

The woman looked into her face for a few moments and then let her eyes go slowly down Martha's body.

"I think I know or can make a guess as to what he is and also to what he has done."

Martha was aware of her face flushing. How could this woman know…how could anyone? Surely there was nothing to be seen yet…she wanted to explain.

"But he said that…we were going to…we…"

The woman smiled but such a smile that had nothing but cruelty in it as if whatever hurts her own life had given her could be eased by it.

"Well you will have learned a lesson in life now. A young man will say many things, many fine and beautiful things when the wanting is in him but in the new day they are gone…as he has done."

Martha could not say any more. There was no way of explaining to this bitter woman that Matthew was so different, that he was true, and yet…he was gone. She felt sick and knew that all she could do was to leave that woman and that place, so she turned and began to run back the way she had come.

She ran until she could run no more and then she walked.
Her mind was in confusion. There were her fears about Matthew and why he had not come, why he had gone away. Where? Why? Could it possibly be true, those hateful things the woman in the village had said. But there was also the other thing she had said, the thing she had guessed or even known. How much longer before people in her own village saw…before they knew? True she had told Jared, but had he told Anne or anyone else. Surely not, or else Anne would have spoken of it.
She had her answer when she reached the cottage and walked inside. Jared was not there, and Anne just looked at her angrily. "And where have you been off to? She snapped. "Don't you know there's work to be done."
Martha made no answer other than a quiet apology and then leaving off her cloak began on her chores as if it were just another day.

………................................………

Martha could not sleep. She lay awake and thought about Matthew. She had believed him. She had trusted him. If he had wanted to leave her after what she had told him about Jared and the baby, then she knew that he would have been honest with her. Why else would he have made plans to meet her at their special place and go away with her to start a new life together. She knew that there was no-one she could ask; no-one she could turn to who could help her find him. She felt that if only she could see him and talk with him then if he had truly changed his mind, she would accept it, but she had to know…to understand. Suddenly she had a strange thought. Instead of laying in her bed with her mind in turmoil, she would go back to their place by the river, a place where they had been happy…perhaps there she would have better thoughts.

Though she knew that a second mornings absence could only bring her more trouble from Anne she could not help herself and so as the dawn was slowly breaking she quietly rose and dressed, leaving the cottage whilst Jared and Ann were still asleep just as she had done the day before. The difference was that then her heart had been full of hope and expectation, now she felt only a sense of loss and bewilderment. The village was quiet, and she quickly took the road that led towards the woods and the river.

Whereas yesterday there had been just a scent of autumn, today there seemed to be a stronger breeze and a chill to the air.
As every hurried step went by, she half expected to see Matthew in front of her, and as every moment passed her fear and disappointment grew.
 After a little while she came to their place by the

large oak tree. With a sudden stab of pain she remembered the times she and Matthew had met here. She looked at where he had carved their entwined initials and the heart design into the bark of the tree. She moved closer and let her finger slowly and tenderly trace their outlines.

"Martha"

She turned around hoping against reason that he was there but the small clearing by the river was empty, it had only been her wishful mind or the wind through the leaves. She felt drained and so tired that she decided to rest for a while before returning to the village. She sat down, resting her back against the tree. She could feel the tears that she had been holding in since the day before starting to come and closed her eyes trying to find some comfort and peace in the sounds of the place…of their place…the sound of bird song, and something else…

Water. There was water. Running and swirling. It was calling her, it was claiming her and rising above her head. She opened her eyes with a start. It was nothing. Somehow, she must have fallen asleep for a while and dreamed it. Of course…she was so close to the river. She could hear it now. She slowly got to her feet. She suddenly felt so cold and shuddered. The place that had been theirs, that had been so special felt somehow different. There was pain here. There was evil. She quickly turned around and began to walk back towards the village.

21
Alone.

The weeks that followed seemed like a dream to Martha. During the days she was able to carry out all her housework as if everything was usual. It was the nights that were different though. At night she would lay in bed in her small room and turn over and over in her mind the events since that last time she had been with Matthew.

She knew that every day was a day nearer to the time when she would have to tell Anne. There had been times in those weeks when Anne had looked at her strangely, especially when she seemed tired or slow in doing her work. As for Jared, any looks he did give her were only what they had been all of her life...hatred. There were nights when she thought that the easiest thing to do would simply be to run away. She would make whatever plans and preparations she could and then one early morning just slip out of the cottage and go to...?
That was where the thoughts came up against the reality. She knew that there was no place she could go to in her condition.
There were times when she sensed that Anne was in one of her softer moods and she almost felt that she might be able to tell her. She had no doubts about Jared's threats and so she tried to think of some story that would not make what she had known with Matthew into something dirty and cheap. She knew what the truth was and also knew how she would suffer if she was forced to spend the rest of her life

living with a never-ending lie.

Time and nature took the decision out of her hands as early one morning as she was sweeping the floor, she suddenly dropped the broom and rushed outside where she bent over and vomited into the lane. As she took gulps of air and stood up straight, she turned round to see Anne standing in the doorway and looking at her no longer strangely but with the certainty of knowledge before turning away and walking back into the cottage.
After a few minutes Martha came back inside to see Anne seated at the table, her face expressionless, holding out a mug of small ale towards her.
"Drink this, sit down, and then tell me."
Martha took the drink and swallowed a few sips. She did not know what to say, what story to tell that might be believed. All she did know was what she could not and must never say. She brought the mug to her mouth and made a show of drinking some more to gain even a few more moments.
Anne reached across and took the mug out of her hands. "I said tell me."
Martha closed her eyes so as not to be able to watch Anne's face as she forced herself to bring out the words.
"I am with child" she said softly.
"I know that" replied Anne "Any fool would now know that. Who is the father?"
Martha felt as if her whole life had somehow led to this point and that everything that would ever happen in the future would also follow from this one moment. With her eyes still firmly closed she

spoke the name. In her mind it was not in answer to Anne's question. It was a desperate call to him wherever he was. "Matthew."
There was a momentary silence.
"And what is he going to do now." demanded Anne.
"I do not know."
"Well what does he say, I thought you had planned to be wed."
Again Martha could only make the same answer. "I do not know."
This time Anne's voice was impatient. "Is he to come here and speak with Jared and me?"
Martha felt the tears begin to run down her cheeks as she spoke the words that seemed to make what had happened more sharply and painfully real than she had been able to accept till now. "He has gone."
Anne was silent. Martha slowly opened her eyes and met her gaze, unsure of what was in it.
Anne stood up and looked down at Martha. She shook her head. "You bloody fool. What am I to tell your brother when he comes home?"
"Tell him whatever you wish." Martha said quietly.

And that evening when Jared did return, Anne told him plainly and simply, her voice without either anger or sympathy. He had looked across the room to where Martha sat silently in the corner.
"So he has gone has he" he said with a half smile on his face. "I knew he were a bad one since that time in the market."
Anne stared at him "What time in the market?"
Jared tried to cover the mistake he knew he'd made and nodded across to Martha. "Oh it were one time

he came over and started talking to her, but I saw him off."

"Tis a pity he took no heed of you then" said Anne "If he had then she might not be in this state."

"Well what's to be done now?" asked Jared.

"There's nothing to be done except for her to wait out her time and have the baby." replied Anne.

"And what then? Another mouth to feed, that will grow up as useless as her."

Martha had lived with Jared's hatred all her life. She had seen it in his face, heard it in his words and felt it at his hands, but only now and for the first time did she understand what pure hatred felt like. She looked at his face with its wicked mocking expression. She saw the puckered damaged skin and the scars that the had given him all those years ago and her one thought was only that she wished she had been able to do more.

She was tired of it all. The lies...the false accusations against Matthew and the certain knowledge that this was all the future would hold for her.

She felt a strange courage springing up inside her. Her life was gone, Matthew was gone. What could the years ahead possibly bring but more pain and sorrow. Rather end it all now. She had known happiness for the briefest time. She had loved and felt herself to be loved. It was over. Now it seemed that there was nothing more that she could lose. Now in this moment she would speak out. She knew that if she did not then she could not face the rest of her life. Jared and Anne were looking at her. There was a tightness in her throat as she struggled to

bring out the words. She summoned the last bit of courage she felt and finally the words came.
"The baby..."
Jared's expression changed to one of shock and he took a step towards her.
She had to speak out before he reached her. Before he stopped her.
Suddenly, and for the first time she felt it. Unbelievable. Unmistakable.
A tiny movement inside her. She gasped and stepped back from Jared. She clasped her hands to her stomach. Anne was looking from Martha to Jared.
"What of the baby?" she demanded.
Martha made no answer as she felt the room begin to spin and she fell to the floor with her hands clasped across her stomach shielding the growing life within her.

When she came to, Martha was in her bed with Anne by her side looking down at her. There was concern in her face but also a question.
"The baby" she asked, "What did you want to say?"
Martha looked beyond Anne to where Jared was standing behind her. If his expression was also one of concern, she knew it was not for her welfare.
"It was nothing" Martha replied. "It was just that I suddenly felt it move."
Anne stared into her eyes and then turned to Jared for a moment before looking back at Martha. "And that was all?"
Martha slowly nodded. "That was all."

22
Martha's time.

February 1609.

The days and months passed, the year turned, and Martha's time came close. The mellow beauty of autumn had long passed, and a harsh and bitterly cold winter gripped the village and surrounding countryside.

Inside the cottage the atmosphere had mirrored the season, becoming ever colder. For Jared, whenever he was away working there was always the fear that one day, he would return to find that Martha had spoken the words of accusation, and though he would deny it, somehow he felt that Anne would know the truth.

For Anne apart from the fact that increasingly there was less work which Martha could do and which fell to her, there was the resentment she felt that she had conceived no child of her own and now was never like to given how things had stood between Jared and her since that night he had called out Martha's name as he roughly thrusted inside her.

…..

For Martha as the baby grew inside her so did the fear of the coming birth increase in her mind. She was finally unable to hold it to herself and so one evening when she was alone with Anne, Jared being as was usual these days at the inn with Ralph, Edward and Thomas, she waited for the moment when Anne was sitting quietly by the fire at rest and sat down next to her.

Anne looked at her as if she had been expecting Martha to ask something of her, be it either advice or help.

"I think...I feel that it is very close now." Martha said.

Anne glanced down at Martha's swollen belly. "It will come when it be ready and the good Lord wills it so."

Martha felt that there were so many questions she wanted to know and yet instead of being able to form them she started to cry. "I am afraid."

"What is it that you fear?" Anne replied. "Is it the pain of birthing?"

Martha nodded. "It is that, but also I feel so alone."

"You will not be alone. I will be there and when your time comes, I shall call for Goodwife Mary. It was she that helped your mother and brought you into the world."

Martha was silent for a moment and then spoke softly as if she did not want to bring the words out. "And my mother died".

Any hardness that was so usual in Anne seemed suddenly to soften. She reached across and took Martha's hand. "That she did" she paused and then continued " But you...you shall live."

…..................................

The following days moved into weeks and Martha thought more and more about Matthew. She imagined a time in the future when she would find out and perhaps come to understand why he had gone. There were even some times when she thought she would look up and he would be standing there in front of her. He would explain...she would understand. All of the misery and fear of the past months would simply vanish and the new life they had planned could begin. She felt such an aching desire to see him...to hear his voice...to be close to him.

The tree! She suddenly felt that there was no other place where she could sense his nearness. Though there was no sense in it and though every step she took caused her pain, she knew that she had to go to the tree.

Martha slowly moved to the door of the cottage. The day was bitter cold and yet somehow, she felt that she had to go outside. She knew her time was very near, but she was overcome by a desire to walk out from the village to what had been their place. Both Anne and Jared were out, and she knew that this could well be the last chance she had to go before the baby came. She was not sure if she could get that far and yet the need in her to do it was stronger than any other thought.

The lanes were empty as she slowly began to walk towards the edge of the village. Her mind was telling her that this was madness, but her heart had an even stronger pull and she carried on.

She paused for a few moments as she passed old Margaret's cottage where she had spent so many happy hours. She missed her company and advice more than ever and knew that had Margaret been alive then she would have been there to help her. The cottage had been taken over by other people who had made repairs to the thatch and walls, but for all that, Martha had loved it as it was, and more so the wise old woman who had lived there.

By the time she reached the edge of the village she knew that it had been a mistake and yet still she walked on. She could not help thinking how this time would have been had Matthew been by her side. They would have already started that new life which now seemed to have been just a dream. She wondered where they would have gone and how they would have lived.

There had been so many times in the past months when she had wanted to hate him. Those times had come, and they had gone. What she desperately needed was to know...to understand. She stopped, overcome with pain. She wanted only to turn back now but it was as if that were impossible. She tried to think how much further it would be if she walked on. She knew that even if she got there then she would be unable to get back. Each step was an agony. She began to be angry with herself for putting the unborn baby at risk. What matter how it had been conceived. It was hers. It would always be hers.

She was aware of a sudden warmth between her legs. She stopped and with a sudden helpless panic, she knew that her time had arrived.

Now she did turn around and begin to walk back towards the village. The pains had started to come strongly and though she knew she had to hurry she was hardly able to put one foot in front of the other.

She started to cry with the frustration and the fear that she would not be able to get safely back and that she would simply collapse and have to give birth alone on the cold and dirty track, and just like her mother...she would die.

For the briefest of moments the thought that there would be an end to it all seemed almost comforting, but then she felt the push of the life within her waiting to be born. Somehow that thought gave her some strength and she struggled on. She knew if she could even get to the outskirts of the village there was sure to be someone who might help her. She looked to the sky where she could see the twisting smoke of fires. She knew that she must be getting closer, but the pains were coming faster now and she could think of nothing else.

The track started to bend around, and she knew that she was almost there. Martha prayed for that last bit of strength that would carry her through to safety. She came to a sudden stop, overcome with pain. She knew this was the end and that she had no more to give. She moved towards the bend and slowly began to sink to the ground. With a flash of recognition she suddenly realized that she had fallen outside what had been Margaret's cottage. "Help me...please help me." she cried through the pain and fear. There was no answer and she closed her eyes in a final and accepting resignation of whatever was to be.
"Don't be afeared child."
It was Margaret's voice. It was unmistakable and

she was aware of a comforting warmth spreading through her entire body easing the pain. She slowly opened her eyes praying that she had not been mistaken and that she would see that wonderful old face again.
It was not there...but as she lay on the ground, she looked down the lane to where unbelievably she could see Anne running towards her.

23
The Baby.

Martha lay on the bed, Goodwife Mary White holding her by the hand and with Anne by her side. The pains were closer and stronger now. Martha found that somehow, she was able to bear the physical pain easier than that of the possibility that like her mother before her, these might be her final moments of life, and how she could die without anyone knowing the truth. How would it be if she was gone and what people remembered of her was false. She looked at Anne. Could she tell her? Would she be believed? "Anne…I must tell you…" her words were cut short as an excruciating pain overtook her. Anne's face was hard although strangely enough her hands were gentle as she wiped the sweat from Martha's brow.
"Do not speak. It is not a time for talking, just work for the child…it's almost coming."
"I am feared that I will die and that no-one will know "
Anne glanced quickly at Goodwife Mary.
"There be nothing to know" she said sharply "There be nothing that I want to hear, just put your energies into the baby ".
Martha had not the strength or will to argue. This could be as it had been for her own mother in this very same cottage all those years ago. These could be her last moments of life and if she could do nothing else then she would try and help her unborn baby into the world. The pain was overwhelming and yet she felt that there was also strength, some

unknown force that was with her, helping her. It was neither Anne nor Goodwife Mary, who both just wanted the whole business over and done with. She closed her eyes and tried to push through the fear and the pain and concentrate only on whatever the force that seemed to be supporting and encouraging her was.

The baby

As she made the final strained effort and the baby came, she realized what and who the force had been.

…..

In the evening Jared returned to the cottage to find Anne sitting by the fire and gently cradling a baby in her arms. At first, she seemed not to notice him, so intent was she in looking down at the child and stroking its head. Suddenly she became aware of his presence and looked at him. He moved towards them fearful of any emotion that might show on his face. At first Anne held the baby even closer, almost protectively and then slowly held her up. "It's a girl." she said quietly.

Jared momentarily felt a strange rush of satisfaction that after all these childless years with Anne he had proved, even if only to himself, that he was a man whose seed could make a child. He glanced at the baby immediately noticing the covering of its fine yet dark hair, and then at Anne in whose eyes he could now only see questions. Suddenly a hope sprang up that surely it should be Martha sitting

nursing the baby and did that mean that... he looked around.
Anne immediately understood and answered his unspoken thought.
 "She be sleeping." she said and turned her face back down to the baby she held tightly in her arms.

24
Wilkin.

February 1609.

Martha slowly walked through the village; the baby wrapped tightly in a shawl held close to her. It was four days since the birth. She was still sore and every step she took sent sharp stabs of pain through her body. She was aware of the glances she attracted from any of the villagers that saw her. None came to congratulate her or to look at the baby. She was dreading speaking to Henry Wilkin. The last time she had done so had been outside Margaret's cottage after she had died and when he had refused to let her say her farewell to the old woman. The only other time was all those years before when she had pleaded with him to protect her from her father and he had turned away. She tried to put those bitter memories out of her mind as she came through the gate and began to walk down the path that went through the tree lined graveyard towards the church door.

She felt her courage begin to fail and stood still for a few moments. She looked across to the side and realized that she had stopped only a few paces away from the grave of her mother. She turned from the path and walked over to the small wooden cross. She held the baby close as she softly whispered the few words. "See mother, this is my child. No matter how she came into being, I shall hold and love her, as much for a remembrance of you as for anything

else." She suddenly stopped and turned. Had she heard her name? She glanced around and then looked up towards the top of the church tower where the cockerel weather vane was moving with the wind that had sprung up. There was nothing.
 Once more she thought she heard something. She looked up again and saw a single bird flying around the top of the tower. There was something about it that suddenly threw her mind and thoughts back to her own Beth. Of course it couldn't be, that had been years before, and she would probably not still be living....And yet.

She watched as the bird continued to circle the tower, and as she watched, any fears she had about facing Henry Wilkin seemed to leave her and be replaced by a calm determination. She kissed the baby, turned away from the grave and walked on down the winding path to the church door. She grasped the iron handle and turned it.

As she entered the church Martha held the baby even closer to her. She moved slowly up the aisle towards the vestry. She gently knocked on the door. There was no answer and so she knocked again and then slowly opened it. Henry Wilkin was seated at his desk writing. He looked up with an expression of annoyance at having been disturbed.
"I am sorry" said Martha "I did knock but there was no answer."
"There was no answer because I am writing my sermon for this Sunday" he replied curtly. His eyes narrowed as he saw who it was that had broken his concentration and thoughts. "What is it you want?"

"If it please you…"

The priest laid down his quill and looked sternly at Martha and the baby she cradled in her arms.

"I have known you since you were a child and you have never pleased me. I know well who you are girl. The whole village knows who, and what you are. I say again…what do you want?"

Martha turned the baby towards him. "I want this child to be received into Christ's mercy and love. I want her to be baptized. She will be called Elizabeth in memory of my mother."

Wilkin's face clouded with anger "You must know that is impossible…the child is born by sin."

Martha looked into his eyes and knew with certainty that he would not change his mind. She saw in his cold hard face the same look that she remembered from years before when as a frightened child after she had scarred Jared, she had begged for help and shelter in this very church and from this same priest. That time he had turned away, leaving her to be taken back by her father to the worst beating of her life. As he was then...so he was now.

"Please, I do not ask this for me" Martha pleaded "I ask it for the child. If there be sin, then how can it be hers?"

Wilkin made no answer other than to take up his quill, look back down at the paper in front of him and continue writing.

Martha turned and leaving the vestry walked back down the aisle and out of the church.

25
The Church.

That Sunday as she slowly awoke from a night of restless and troubled sleep, Martha knew that she could not go to the church for the service.
She could not be there whilst Henry Wilkin spoke his sanctimonious words and whilst all the villagers looked at her with expressions that ranged from condemnation to disgust. She told Anne and Jared that she was feeling unwell and would stay at home. She looked out of the window to a cold day that surely threatened snow.
She saw birds flying overhead, black against the brooding and overcast winter sky.

She felt lost and abandoned. She was seventeen years old and it seemed as if the entire world was against her and the only person who had ever showed kindness and love towards her had proved false. Even now she found it hard to believe that all Matthew's words had meant nothing and that he had gone. There were times when she turned around quickly at the sound of footsteps, half expecting to see him, to be given an explanation...to be told that all would now be well. She gently lifted the baby from its cot and moved over to the hearth where she sat and cradled it. She thought how different it would have been if this had been the child that she and Matthew would have had. She could feel the tears welling up and starting to run down her face.

She looked at the baby and suddenly any feelings

she might have had of self-pity seemed to vanish and instead turn to a deep anger. She alone knew the truth of this child and whatever blame there could be was neither hers nor above all this gentle innocent life nestling in her arms. Surely it was Christ himself who had said "Suffer little children to come unto me". Suddenly it was as if something else...someone else had come inside her and was taking over her actions, guiding and forcing her. She rose and wrapped the baby in a shawl, and without another thought walked out of the cottage and into the freezing cold morning. She stood for a few moments outside. She looked down the empty lane that led out of the village and towards the open countryside. She held the baby closer to her. She took a deep breath, turned and began to walk towards the church.

Inside the church Henry Wilkin had just climbed the few steps into the pulpit and having looked around at all the faces obediently and expectantly turned towards him had begun to speak. He was pleased with their attention. He knew this was to be one of his good sermons. He had spent much time and effort on it, though with a sudden flash of irritation he remembered the interruption caused by that girl and her bastard. No matter...he had put her in her place and could concentrate his attention solely on the waiting faithful.

"I ask for the blessing of God on my child."

The priest stopped in mid-sentence and stared

toward where the door of the church had been opened. Slowly, at first, just a few, and then the whole congregation turned to where Martha stood by the font cradling her baby . She looked around at all the people and then straight at Wilkin.

"I beg you. Will you not baptize this child and bring her into God's care and love?"

The priest glared at her. "I have told you…the child has been born into sin. This has been your doing and you must accept the consequences."

The congregation gave a collective gasp as instead of being silenced, Martha made bold enough to answer in a firm voice.

"And if it were sin, then could I have been alone?"

Wilkin felt the colour in his face rising with his anger.

"No, you were not alone," he answered, "But all here know that the one who shared your sin has not even been honest enough to own to it and has abandoned both you and the child."

Martha looked around the church at the angry and accusing faces, she looked back to where the priest in all his robed authority stood in the pulpit, and then she looked upwards to where the cross hung behind the altar. Again she remembered the time six years before when she had stood in this church and looked towards that same cross for shelter and help. There had been none then and she knew there would be none now. Where was kindness and charity? Where was God's love?

It was as if something had broken within her. That as if the pain and shame were not enough, to have to stand here in this place of God and hear the evil false words spoken against Matthew who had only ever shown her love and respect, was the final insult she could no longer bear. In this holy place she would speak the truth that both she and God knew. She took a deep breath and spoke out in a clear and strong voice.

"It is true that the one who shared " she paused for a moment " The one who brought my sin upon me, has abandoned me and this innocent child." she took a deep breath, " But that one is here among you." She looked towards where Jared sat next to Anne, his face ashen. " The only man who has ever known me sits there…my brother Jared."

There was a moment of pure silence, as the congregation looked over to Jared, his face now a mask of shock and disbelief, then he stood up. "She is lying…she wants to throw the guilt anywhere other than the boy who has run away rather than marry her and own to the child. Why else has he disappeared from his village?"

There were murmured voices of agreement from all around the church. Over the preceding months it had become local knowledge and gossip how a young potter from a nearby village had suddenly left his uncle's home and not been seen since. Martha closed her eyes and listened to the whispers and mutterings of the people around her, and above them the angry grating voice of Jared, now working himself into a righteous fury, as he addressed the congregation. "You all know how strange she is, of the way she was born, taking the life of my mother."

he pointed to his face "And doing this to me."

A hush settled over the church as Martha moved up the aisle towards the pulpit and the altar. She held the baby upwards towards the cross and cried out. "What I have said here today, I swear to be true. As God is my witness."
Jared's face was now contorted with rage and he made to move towards her but was held back by Anne. The raised and angry voice of Henry Wilkin was heard above the noise of the congregation as he glared down at Martha and the baby from the pulpit. " How dare you! It is not for such a wicked sinner as you to talk about God."

The words seemed to spill out of Martha even without her mind having thought about them. The power of her voice seemed to grow and carry to the furthest corners of the church. There was an edge to it that chilled all who heard her. Still cradling the baby she moved her right arm and pointed at Jared and then in a slow sweeping motion let her gesture carry around the entire congregation finally letting it stop at Henry Wilkin.
"If I cannot talk of God…then I will talk of the devil. May he take you Priest, and all here who think and believe as you do...May he take you and damn you"

It was a moment frozen in time and then there was pandemonium. Henry Wilkin screamed out "Blasphemy" and made the sign of the cross. Several people started shouting, and then at first from a single voice and then by others…the word. "Witchcraft"

The Priest's voice was choking with anger. "Seize her." he shouted. "She will be made to answer for this."

Jared's friends Edward and Thomas who were nearest to her, moved from their pews and took hold of Martha.

Jared felt himself overwhelmed with a mixture of fear and hate. He looked away from Martha and towards Anne. What he saw in her face shocked him more than Martha's words had done. He looked around the congregation and found in other faces the same questioning look that had been in Anne's. His mind was whirling from one thought to another. He felt…no, he knew that people were looking to him to say something. He took a deep breath and then shouted out across the church

"She is possessed and evil…We must send for the Witchfinder"

There was a moments shocked silence and then his call was taken up by first one and then others. "Send for the Witchfinder".

The voice of the priest sounded out above the noise "Take her and keep her well secured and guarded. We will indeed send to Exeter. She will be made to answer for the evil words she has spoken today.

Edward and Thomas roughly dragged Martha, still desperately clutching at her baby out of the church. Jared stood still and looked around him. It seemed that now Martha had been taken out then all eyes in the church had turned towards him. There would be questions... perhaps even more accusations. He knew he had to get away, for however short a time. He stumbled to his feet and rushed towards the door. He suddenly stopped realizing what his panic would look like. He tried to calm himself and hoping that he could hide the fear in his voice called out.

"Since the witch made her false claim against me then I will go for the Witchfinder."

26
Flight.

The small village lock up that stood by the side of the market place hall was occupied with a vagrant who had been accused of trying to steal a horse, and so Martha was taken back to her own cottage with Thomas and Anne set to watch over her for the coming night. Jared had taken the horse and set off to Exeter within the hour. To his relief Anne had neither wanted to question him nor even speak or look towards him. The people of the village went to their homes all excitedly talking about what they had witnessed. It would be the next day before Jared and the Witchfinder could return and all speculated about how events would turn when they did arrive.

…...........................

The dull winter daylight had faded, and the cottage was lit only by the firelight and a couple of cheap candles which spluttered and flickered.
Martha sat in the corner still cradling the baby. Anne had not spoken, and Thomas had been content to sit by the fireside and accept the mugs of ale that Anne had been offering him. He had never known her to be this free with their drink on any past occasions he had been in the cottage and by the time night was falling, the drink and the warmth of the fire was beginning to make him feel drowsy.

Thomas drained the last of the contents of his mug and wiped his mouth on his sleeve. "Do you have more ale?" he asked.

"You've finished all that was in the jug." said Anne

"This keeping watch is a thirsty business." said Thomas. "Are you sure there be no more in the pantry?"

Anne gave him an angry look "I said that jug was the last of it "she answered.

For a moment Thomas looked downcast at the prospect of staying through the night with these two...one a probable witch and the other a plain and harsh shrew. He was taken by surprise when Anne spoke.

"Why do you not go to the tavern then and drink your fill?"

"You know why" he replied sullenly, "Jared told me to stay here with you and the witch."

Anne gave him a mocking look. "And is he then your master…do you have to do what Jared commands?"

Thomas looked down into his empty mug "Of course not, but he said…"

"Never mind what he said…do you not think that I can guard a slip of a girl and her baby while you have a few drinks?...surely you'll be gone for but an hour"

Thomas thought for a few moments. What harm could it do...in the tavern there would be drink and some good company rather than stay in this silent and oppressive room. He slowly got to his feet and moved towards the door.

"Well I will take your offer and be back later so you can have some sleep. Jared and the Witchfinder will not be back before the morrow."

Anne nodded. "Go then...I shall see you later."

The door closed behind Thomas, and for a few moments there was silence in the room as the candle and light from the fire threw moving shadows against the wall. Martha had laid the now sleeping baby in its small cot which she had moved closer to the fire. She turned and saw that Anne was looking at her with what seemed to be a mixture of anger…and of something else that Martha could not fully understand, and then she spat the words out.
"You cursed him…in front of the whole village, you cursed him. How could you speak those words to any Christian, let alone your own brother?"
For Martha the time for lying was now past, come what may. She took a breath and looked directly at Anne.
"The words I spoke were true. It was Jared."
Anne's face was set as she angrily responded, "I do not believe you…when did it happen?"
"It was the time your father was hurt, and you went away to him."
Anne was looking at Martha with a different expression…was there any chance that it could be belief? she continued "Do you not remember…I had a bruise to my face, and I told you I had fallen"
"So did you lie then as you are lying now?"
"Yes…I did lie then, but I do not lie now. I swear it."

Anne did not speak for a few moments. She looked towards the baby laying in its cot. Why could that child not have been hers? Everything would have been so different. God knows in the early years it had not been for want of trying. Now though, she knew that Jared felt no desire for her and in truth she felt none for him…in fact she never had. It had been a marriage of convenience for them both and the only thing that would have made it other than something to regret would have been a child. A child like the beautiful baby that now lay sleeping a few feet away. Was the accusation true? Anne knew Jared's nature and she knew it could well be.

"What does any of that matter now " Anne said.

"It matters because it is the truth." answered Martha quietly.

"Only God will know whether that be so " Anne said " And He will also have heard the words of blasphemy and curse that you spoke in his own House."

Martha did not know what more to say and so remained silent. Anne looked at her and the bitterness in her face seemed to soften for a moment, "Do you know what will happen when the Witchfinder arrives? You will not be able to remain silent then."

Martha could find no words with which to make an answer. In truth, she did not know what would happen, but she felt it would be bad…very bad. Anne continued to look at her but now in a strange way as if she were unsure of how to speak the thoughts that now came. Finally she spoke. "Jared will be returning tomorrow with the Witchfinder. Do you want them to find you still here?"

For a moment Martha didn't understand. Of course if there were any other way…but Jared had left her in Anne and Thomas's charge and…and Thomas was gone. Anne had sent him away. She began to understand and even to hope. But why would Anne offer her a chance to escape, was she thinking of Martha…or of Jared…did it matter?

"Leave now " Anne said firmly.

Martha looked across to Anne in disbelief of the words she had just heard.

"But Jared has told you to keep me here until he…"she paused "until they return."

"You leave me to worry about Jared. I will say you escaped whilst I slept and anyway the blame will be part upon Thomas who could not keep from a drink"

The thought of escape and a new start, a new life flooded through Martha. There was no time to think or to plan. If she were to go then she must leave immediately, just a few minutes to gather some food and some warm clothes and…

"Well" Anne snapped "Are you going to go, or do you wish to remain here?"

Martha was overcome by a feeling of gratitude and the sudden hope that there was still a possibility of getting away and making a new start.

"We will go…and thank you Ann for the chance to..."

Anne gave her a cold and hard look.

"I said I would allow you to leave. The baby stays here...with me"

Martha was struck almost speechless as she suddenly realized what Ann was offering.

Anne's voice was now full of anger,

"Think for a moment you foolish girl. How far do

you think you could travel with a baby in your arms. Where would you go? what would you do? If the child stays, she will have shelter and she will have a home."

Martha knew and understood the truth of Anne's words and yet at the same time she knew it was impossible. She would never leave her baby. Her mind was spinning. Why did Ann want her baby, did she know, had some part of her always known or was it the words Martha had spoken in the church? She tried to think back and remember how Anne had reacted, but she could only recall the burning hatred in Jared's twisted face. Her throat was suddenly very dry…

She rose from her chair as if in a dream and moved over to the table. She reached out towards the stoneware jug and began to pour herself some water into the mug at its side. Suddenly her grasp on the handle tightened and she spun around and lifting her arm high brought the jug crashing down against Anne's head. There was a sickening sound as the jug shattered and Anne dropped without a word from her chair onto the floor. Martha looked down as the water mixed with the blood that was now coming from a gash in Anne's head.

For a few moments Martha was unable to move. She stared down in horror at Anne's body lying still on the floor and looked with a sickened fascination at the blood slowly making a spreading stain. Was she just unconscious? Panic swept through her...there was no movement, no sound.

She quickly moved over to the cot where she snatched her baby up and wrapping a shawl around it and taking Anne's cloak from where it hung by the door rushed out into the street.

She quickly looked around but could see no-one. She was in shock over what she had just done. Was Anne dead or alive? Should she go back and tend to her?

  She looked back through the doorway to where Anne was laying unmoving on the floor and then she looked down at the baby in her arms. She knew what she had to do and immediately began to run down the lane that led over the old bridge and out of the village and to the countryside beyond. Though there was no-one in the streets and lanes she somehow felt that she was being watched from every window, from every doorway. She felt all their eyes upon her and that they all knew what she had done.

She hardly noticed the light snow that had begun to fall and clasping her baby tightly ran without stopping until she halted, panting for breath and felt able to turn and look behind her. No-one. She was not being pursued.

She was alone. Behind her lay the night covered village. Behind her lay the inn where Thomas was drinking ale. Behind her lay the cottage where Anne's blood must surely still be spreading across the floor. She looked towards the open countryside where there might be escape, where she might find safety.

There was nothing she could do. She was alone.

Matthew was gone and there was no one to help her. Thomas would soon be returning from the inn to find her gone. Anne was perhaps dead…
And…

The Witch finder was coming.

27
Escape.

February 1609.

She had awoken as if from a dream but that was in reality the worst nightmare of her life. It had been hours since Martha had left the cottage and run out into the night. The weather had worsened, and the snow had fallen almost as if in divine punishment for the words she had spoken in the church and above all for what she had done to Anne.
She had come under the shelter of the woods to tend the baby and to find a couple of hours of rest. She was tired and she was scared. She knew that she had done wrong but as she looked down at the baby suckling at her breast, she also knew that there had been no other choice.

After a few moments when the baby's hunger had been satisfied, she stood up and looked around. She felt disorientated. Had she slept and if so, for how long had it been? The sky was still dark so surely it can only have been for a short while. She started to retrace her steps out of the wood and back towards the path. Her boots were soaked through and every step in the snow seemed to be so hard. The landscape around her looked entirely different with its covering of white but she thought...she hoped, that she'd remembered the way.
 As she walked a sudden panic came to her. Would the path be the safest choice? Surely that would be the way that anyone following her would take, but if

she went further into the woods then where would that lead her?

The woods seemed to hold the promise of cover and safety but the track towards the city would be quicker. There was no time to think. What she had to choose, if not for her sake then for the baby's was speed and the chance of reaching some sort, any sort of shelter from the cold and the snow.

Within a few minutes she had found the way back to where she was able to rejoin the track and continue, hoping against hope that she would soon see some sign of habitation where she might find shelter if only for a while. The track had had begun to rise and the climb was taking the last of her strength. She thought that she would allow herself a short stop and rest when she reached the brow of the hill. The snow was becoming heavier. She held the baby even tighter beneath her now soaking wet cloak, put her head down and pushed forward against the wind and the swirling snow, held up by the promise of stopping within a few minutes. She offered a silent prayer to God and whatever other ancient spirits might be looking down on her in this place and as if in answer she raised her head and saw that she had come to the top of the hill.

She looked as far ahead as she could see. The countryside was simply an empty blanket of white. She turned around to look back at what seemed the endless way she had come and realized with a gasp of fear that behind her the dawn was slowly beginning to lighten the sky.

Again she prayed, this time aloud "Dear God please help us…you know I have done no wrong, whatever might be said against me. You know that the accusations spoken are false..." she paused remembering what had happened in the cottage "You know I would not have harmed Ann had she let me leave with the baby. I could not give her up. It was not just Anne; I would not have had her remain in a house with Jared...not to have the years I had" she shuddered as the other memory came back to her "Not to ever risk that for her."
She closed her eyes hoping that a merciful God would heed her prayers and offer help. She opened them slowly and realized that her prayers were answered. Back down the track perhaps two or three miles away through the still thickly falling snow she saw what must be a cart. Surely the carter would help her and the child, what man could refuse on a night like this, and even if he were only going to the next village, she would at least be able to rest for a while.

There had been a bend further down the track and she now lost sight of the cart. She wondered if perhaps she should retrace her steps and go towards it, but she remembered that there had been no turnings that she had passed and though she could no longer see the cart there was no other track than this and all she had to do was wait. Perhaps death did not always win…
She waited for a few minutes knowing that the cart would also be finding the snow covered track difficult. There was one final moment when she

knew that she had to take the decision to wait or to press on by herself. She looked at her baby and also knew that if there were even the smallest chance that she could find help then that was all she could do.

As she looked back down the track the dawning light showed not only that the cart had come into sight again and was by now half way up the long hill but that all her prayers had just been hopeless words thrown against the wind. It was not her deliverance that came closer, but her capture. For by the same light that had whitened the sky, she saw that the cart held four men who had looked to the top of the hill and seen where she stood, and as surely as they could see and recognize her, then just as surely did she know who they were.
She knew with an ice cold and fearful certainty that… It was Jared.

28
One step too fast.

She could not understand. How could he have got to Exeter and back so quickly? Had he found Anne...was she dead? Martha's mind was overwhelmed by fear and utter exhaustion and could not think of anything other than escape and the safety of her baby. If she stayed where she was, in a short while they would reach her. If she ran onwards, the horse drawn cart would finally overtake her. She looked away and across the open country. There seemed to be the outline of some woods a little way to the right.

The snow blanketed landscape confused her. Were these the same woods that she had sheltered and fallen asleep in? She could not be sure. The fear, the weariness, the panic had all seemed to join together. She had lost sense of place and also time. She tried to think clearly and to make a decision, but it was impossible.

She knew that the cart could not easily follow her if she left the track and if she could reach the woods then she might have a chance. Immediately she began running across the rough and uneven snow-covered ground. Somehow her tiredness had left her, and she felt a new strength in her legs as she began to make her way towards the trees.

She did not look back hoping that her sudden change of direction might not immediately cause the men to abandon the horse and cart and follow her on foot. Her fear seemed to give her speed and within a few minutes she had gained the shelter of the woodland. Still she did not dare to look back and just continued running ever deeper through the trees.

After what seemed an endless time she stopped, panting for breath. She knew she was at the limit of her strength now and that even for the sake of the baby she had no more in her. The woods around her were denser than before and the weak wintery pre-dawn light had begun to filter through them.

She listened carefully but couldn't hear anything other than the sounds of the birds. She wanted to believe that the men had given up and returned to the village. She thanked a merciful God to have seen her through the night and given her another chance to escape towards the city, towards safety. But which way was the city? she knew that she could not risk going back to the track, but what other escape was open to her. The woods that had given her safety and shelter now seemed only to mock her. There were no signing posts, there was no path, and indeed if she was to find one, surely that would be where they would be waiting. She knew that as the light of the dawn would have come from the east then the city must be the opposite way, and yet to walk towards the fast disappearing darkness felt so wrong. Perhaps if she waited. No, she thought, there was nothing to be gained by any delay, the tiredness and fear of the last day and night had drained everything from her, she knew she must go on without any delay. She slowly began to walk towards the place that her heart told her

would take her towards the city.
An hour passed, though to her tired and aching body it seemed much longer, and what light there was to be on that freezing cold winters day had arrived. Though she knew she must hurry, every few steps and every few moments she stopped and listened. The woods seemed to be getting denser and harder to walk through with the twisted roots of the trees causing her to stumble and making her fear for the baby's safety.
Suddenly…A sound !
She stopped and listened. Perhaps it was only her imagination and her fear. She heard it again. It was not the men.
It was the unmistakable barking of Edward's dog.

It was coming from ahead; from the direction she was heading. Of course they would have guessed that she'd try and reach Exeter, it was so obvious to her now, but what could she do? The only possible route was neither ahead nor back but off in the other direction. She clasped the baby tightly and began to run. After just a few minutes she knew that she'd made the wrong choice as the ground beneath her feet became both rougher and she was aware that she was running uphill. She stopped. She must go back and take the other direction, wherever it might lead it could not be harder than this. Just a few steps and with a sickening feeling in her stomach she realized that she could now hear not just Edward's dog but the voices of the men.
 She turned back again and started up the hill. There was now a pounding in her head and a tightness in

her chest. If it were just her she knew she would stop now and let it all finish however it would, but there was the baby, and she knew she would run as long as there was breath left in her body, for as long as she could. But there, a little way ahead there seemed to be an end to the denseness of the woods, perhaps there might be some way of escape if she came into the clear and open countryside. With the last of her strength and will she began to run faster. One step too fast…one step taken without looking…one step.

As she fell and rolled against the trunk of a tree, she shielded the baby in her arms taking the full force of the impact. For a few moments she lay stunned and then she willed herself to get to her feet and carry on. Three more steps and her left ankle gave way beneath her, forcing her down to the ground again. The sounds of her pursuers was clearer now. There was no choice, there had to be one last effort. She dragged herself to her feet and started to move as fast as she was able towards where the trees ended. Each limping step flooded her body with pain, but she knew that each step also perhaps brought her closer to escape. Another couple of minutes, another few steps, a last few moments of hope.

And then she was clear. The woods were behind her, the men were behind her, and ahead…

Ahead there was no hope as with a sudden and shocking horror it came to her that there was no escape. In the confusion of having left the track through the snow shrouded countryside, ahead of her were only the cliffs of Branscombe with their sheer terrifying drop down to the rocks and the sea.

She turned around and saw that the men too had come through the woods. Though there was no sense in it she still moved away from them even though it was towards to cliff's edge. Then finally she knew that there was nowhere else to go.

29
The Cliff.

She stopped.
The four men were now slowly walking towards her and had spread out so that she could only remain where she was or move back closer to the edge. The man slightly in front held up his hand and motioned for the others to stay back although he continued to move towards her. A weak and thin light was now creeping across the dark sky but even before she could fully see him, she knew who it was. It was the one who had led the pursuit, the one who had cursed her and called for the witch finder, the one who had always hated her and would take her child...Jared.

She knew that she was alone. She closed her eyes for a moment and her mind was filled with hopelessness and also the fear of what would now happen. They would take her back to the village. The Witch finder would come. There would be questions, accusations and apart from what had happened in the church there would be the inevitable and inescapable punishment for what she had done to Anne.
She opened her eyes and looked at Jared as he moved closer and she saw the expression on his face. She had thought that she knew all of his looks, be they anger, contempt or hatred but now she saw something that was worse...he was smiling and was now holding out his arms towards her. His voice too seemed to have a different tone, not angry nor

threatening, as she had known it all her life, but quietly calm, and somehow, that scared her more than anything else.

"Come now sister, there's nowhere else to run to. Think of the child…would you take her life as well ?"

"What would you have me do Jared. Would you have me surrender to the Witch finder that I might be taken to the river and put to the test to see if I do sink or swim, either being the death of me. Would you have me cruelly used until I would confess to anything so that the pain be ended. Would you see me hanged; would you see me burned ?"

Jared moved a step closer. "The law must take its course, but the child is blameless, will you take her to damnation with you?" he answered, still with the same cruel fixed smile.

Beyond all Martha's pain and fear, a question came to her mind that she knew that had to be asked.

"And what of Anne? God knows I did not mean to harm her."

Jared was momentarily silent as if thinking what answer would serve his purpose. "Do not you worry about her. She will recover…and she will be there to see you being punished for your wrongs. She will be there to see you hanged for the witch you are."

The light was increasing now. The new day was beginning and for Martha it held nothing but hopelessness. She felt the fight and the will slowly draining out of her. Anne was not dead, perhaps she would be given a fair hearing, there might be a chance of some mercy and at least the child would be safe. At her back she could feel the emptiness, she could hear the waves pounding against the rocks far below. She nodded slowly to Jared who began to move closer, his arms still outstretched. Whatever the future would hold she would accept. She gently passed the baby to Jared, at the same moment feeling a wave of resignation and almost of peace come over her. Jared moved the baby into the crook of his left arm and then in a sudden movement, clenched his right hand and drove it hard into her stomach.

As the shock and pain swept through her she felt her knees give way and crumpled to the ground. Jared reached down to help her up, but instead he was pushing her backwards the last few feet to the edge. She looked up and saw his face now changed. Now the only look it held was pure and bitter hatred. He turned his head to the side. Now there was nothing but cold hard anger in his voice. "Look for one last time on what you did to me and damn you to hell " he cursed as he gave the final push that sent her over the edge through the empty space to the rocks and the waiting sea below.

As Martha went over the cliff edge to what she knew would be her death there was a single momentary flash of recognition as she looked skywards and thought she saw a bird swooping and diving just above her. Time seemed strangely to both slow down and yet also to speed up. There was one final thought.

See me Beth ... I fly.

30
Grace.

The other men now started to come forward and in a few moments were standing next to him as he stood speechless and looking at the edge of the cliff. Jared slowly turned and held the baby towards them
" She gave me the child and then said she would rather die than be taken and face the Witch finder. I tried to reach for her, to save her, but she pulled away." He looked to the faces of the others, unsure of what he saw there. Was it shock…was it fear…was it doubt? "I speak the truth, she chose to die, you all saw it."
The three men looked at one another. It was Edward who spoke. "It was not yet fully light; I don't know whether she fell or jumped or..."
Jared moved closer towards Edward; his face filled with sudden anger. "Or what? What will you swear to when asked? It's done now, she was in fear of the Witchfinder and of what she would have suffered"
"And are you, her brother, so sure that she would have been proved guilty?" said Ralph moving forward to stand between Jared and Edward.
Jared looked from one to the other of the men. "There are none better than I to know what she truly was, and this I would have had to tell at any trial. It be over now, there will be no trial, no judgement, no punishment." he held the baby up "But this is what there is, a new life which Anne and I will raise as our own."
Edward looked at the baby and then at Jared. "And

can we be sure this one is not like its mother "
"We will have to trust in God" answered Jared.
"Let us say amen to that and start our journey back to the village " said Edward, turning away from the others and walking back towards the woods that would lead them back to where the cart had been left.

For the last few miles before they returned to the village there had been silence among the men as the cart slowly moved through the snow-covered tracks. As they finally came to the outskirts of Clanton it was Jared who spoke first.
"A sad day's happenings friends, but perhaps it were God's will it should be so"
The other men remained silent as the cart covered the last few paces before it reached Jared's cottage and he pulled on the reins. He got down and tied the horse to the post waiting for the others to descend. Thomas handed him the baby that seemed to be sleeping and said in a quiet voice. "God's will or no…it were a bad business Jared"
"What could I do" Jared answered angrily ."Shall we not be able to tell of it when the Witchfinder do arrive, do you all want more questions? You know what happened, you know what you saw"
It was Ralph who answered. "We know what you told us"
"Do you call me a liar then?"
Ralph was silent for a moment looking to Thomas and Edward as if seeking confirmation or dissent. Neither of them spoke.
"It's not for me to call you anything" he finally said

"You and the Lord do both know the truth of it, but we all came to help you take her, and whether it was the Witchfinder or the rocks and the sea that would have had her, it was to have been a bad ending."
"Well then, that must be the finish of it." said Jared. He paused for a moment and spoke quietly
"Remember friends, we have all been witness to other things than this…and there were no questions then."
The only answer that now came was the other men turning away and going back to their own homes and lives.

Jared came into the cottage. On a low chair by the side of the fire Anne was sleeping, her head covered with a blood-stained bandage that had been applied by Goodwife Mary who Thomas had rushed for when he had returned from the inn and found Anne laying on the floor.
 Jared looked down at her. God…how had life tied him to this woman. She was no longer beautiful, nor he admitted to himself had she ever been...that didn't worry him, you could always buy beauty, or what passed for it for the price of a few coins in the taverns, but apart from all this it was the sharpness of her tongue that vexed him the most. What was it she wanted from life, what was it she wanted from him? They were who they were and nothing was ever going to change that. The baby stirred in his arms. He moved closer and saw that she was awakening, her eyes were open though she made no sound. He looked from the baby to Anne and wondered if perhaps the child would make a

difference. It was what Anne had always wanted…a child of her own, and through the years when that had failed to happen, he knew that the talk was that it was him, that he had no seed in him. Well here in his arms was the living proof to that falsehood though he could never claim her as his own. Why had it happened this way? All the years of laying with Anne and there had been no blessing of children and yet the one, the only time he had taken Martha she had fallen.

Perhaps this indeed was God's will, a sign that what he'd done had not been wrong, not a sin for which he would suffer in hell. It was surely a sign of his grace. He felt the baby move in his arms and looked down at it again. The words came from his mouth somehow without him knowing.

"Grace. I shall name you Grace."

By the fireside and hearing the sound of his voice Anne stirred and looked at him. "Did you find her? Is she here… is the baby...?" she asked anxiously. Her voice trailed off as Jared moved closer to the light and warmth of the fire and gently, almost as a gift or an offering, held the baby towards her.

"She took her own life" he said quietly "She was so feared of the Witchfinder she went over the cliff to the rocks and the sea."

Anne stared deep into his eyes. After all these years he had thought he knew her but there was now a look on her face that he could not recognize.

Though there was silence between them, it was dense and filled with so many different thoughts and questions that words could not frame nor express. Finally and painfully Anne eased herself up and held out her arms into which Jared moving slowly forward placed the still sleeping baby.

The next morning through an ice cold mist The Witchfinder rode slowly into the village and dismounted by the inn. He had been surprised that the man who had summoned him had chosen to return to the village that previous night rather than make the journey with him the following day, but for sure there was no understanding these country folk. He went inside and was soon told of the previous day's events. There were no questions, no-one's story to confirm or deny. He took a tankard of ale and then set off again for another village four hours hard riding away, the winter's day being short, the weather being foul with snow still on the ground, and there being much of God's good work still to be done.

Part Two
Grace.

31
Different.

1619

In the outside world the history of the age unfolded.
A peace was made with the old enemy Spain,
ending if not decades of enmity then at least the
threat of invasion and war. The word of God was
brought into the English language in the form of a
new translation of the bible. King James's popular
eldest son Henry Prince of Wales died at the age of
eighteen from typhoid fever leaving his younger
brother Charles as heir to the English throne.
In the New world of the Americas a colony was
founded and named for the King… Jamestown.
A great but retired playwright having left London,
ended his days at his country home at Stratford
upon Avon. All this and more, but in the village of
Clanton all stayed much as it ever had been.
Seasons changed, crops were sown and harvested.
People struggled with their daily lives…they
worked, they loved, they laughed, they argued.
Some were born, some died, and all grew older.

……..

Grace reached her tenth birthday, which like all
those preceding it passed uncelebrated and

unmentioned. There were no gifts or kind words. The day was like all those before it. There was work to be done, clothes to mend, wood to be brought in and Anne to be helped with the food...it was just another day.

She was a quiet, serious and slender child, perhaps small for her age. Her complexion was pale, and her face was seldom lightened by a smile. One of the most striking things about her was her raven black hair so very like that of the mother she had never known.

There were many times when she had lain in her bed in the small room at the far end of the cottage and sleep would not come. She had thought about what her mother would have been like, what she would have looked like. So many things, the sound of her voice, the gentle and caring touch of her hand. None of these she would ever know, and it seemed strange to her that she could yearn so much for something she had never had. Yet there were nights when she would dream of that mother. She would see her and speak with her. They would be in a field together. The sun was shining, and her mother would show her things and tell her about the flowers and herbs that grew all around. There would be laughter...there would be love.

In the mornings when she woke, she felt empty and drained and was torn between the comfort the dream had brought and the sadness that it had passed away with the night.

She knew that she was different from the other

children. They all had mothers and fathers, she had only her uncle and Anne. She had grown up hearing the taunts of the village children and the whispers and sly glances of their parents and with the knowledge that her real father was a lad who had run off and that her mother had committed the worst sin, that of suicide. She had been told that was a terrible sin which would have surely damned her mother's soul forever and the only reason that she was not buried in an unmarked and unsanctified grave at the crossroads was that she had been taken by the endless sea.

She was his child. Jared knew that beyond and without doubt, but although everyone in the village remembered Martha, with every passing year Jared felt an ever-growing fear that they would also somehow come to know who her real father was. It was as if within his house there was a constant and growing reminder of the sister who he had hated. The sister who had scarred him. The sister who he had sent to her death over the cliffs. There were even times when Grace looked at him in a strange and almost knowing way as if although a baby, she knew and bore witness to what had happened at Branscombe cliffs.

Perhaps it was even his imagination, but lately it seemed as if Anne who had always treated Grace as the child that she had herself wanted had begun to act differently towards her. A stern look, harsh words, a shortness of temper if she felt the child had done something wrong or not quick enough.

Grace had also felt this change and yet could not begin to understand it. It was as if Anne was somehow upset by her very presence.

It was the evening before market day and Jared and Anne were sitting silently by the fireside. More and more they sat like this without speaking, each with their own thoughts and nursing their own grievances of where life had brought them.
It was Anne who broke the silence. "Tomorrow, take the child to the market with you."
"She be better off here doing work." he replied sullenly
"It's but one day and so any of the work can wait." answered Anne firmly.
Jared looked at her and knew that it was pointless to argue with her when she seemed in this mood.
"Well she'd better be no trouble" said Jared.
"I be sure that if she is, you'll be able to show her otherwise" replied Anne with a knowing look.

32
The Doll

Honiton was the largest market town outside the great city of Exeter and its market day was always crowded with stalls. Grace had never seen such activity. Everywhere there seemed to be such rushing and bustle with all the traders unloading carts and setting out their wares. Everything around her seemed so interesting and new and she wished she were allowed to have a look round but Jared had given her strict instructions not to wander off or to be a nuisance and the one thing she had learned for certain was that to disobey her uncle would bring a very swift and hard response.

For his part Jared concerned himself only with setting out the various wares he'd brought from the village though any time he did come to the market he could not help but remember what had taken place there those years before. He thought of the fight with Matthew and of how he'd been beaten, but any sense of shame that came to him was quickly overcome and erased by also remembering what had come after. He smiled to himself as he cast his mind back to the wood by the riverside and the revenge he'd taken on the young potter.

It had been a slow days business and apart from the fact that he would not be earning much in the way of commission from the Clanton traders whose goods he'd brought to sell, Jared was not looking forward to the welcome he knew he'd receive from

Anne. He knew there would be some way that she would imply that it was his fault.

Finally the cart was loaded, and Jared walked around it to make sure everything was in place and nothing had been left behind. Suddenly he went to his knees making a show of dropping the bag he was carrying. Just as quickly he stood up again having picked up both his own bag and something else that he quickly concealed, and grasping her by the hand, he pulled Grace across the market square and into a small alleyway.

He looked behind him the way they had come and when he felt sure that they had not been followed, brought out from behind his bag a small leather purse. He opened the drawstring and looked inside. He laughed as he then upended the contents of the bag into the palm of his hand. Grace watched as several coins tipped out. He stared at them for a moment before quickly returning them to the purse. He looked down at her. "You're not to speak of this to anyone, do you understand?"

Grace was silent for a moment, Jared roughly grabbed at her arm "I said...do you understand ?"
"Yes " she answered quietly.
"Then that be the better for you then"
"Are we to go home now?" Grace asked.
He looked back towards the market square, feeling the weight of the purse still in his other hand. Yes, he thought, a bit of luck was long due to him. Always the same scratching for a hard living and having to account to Anne for whatever he did make. He deserved a tankard or two of ale before

returning to the angry tongue and sour face of his wife.

He slowly walked back and out of the alley with Grace by his side. They walked over to where the horse and cart stood waiting.

He looked at Grace and nodded towards an inn a few paces away. "I'm going inside for a while, you're to stay out here and wait. Don't you dare move or wander off or I'll take my belt to you, do you understand? "

Grace looked up at him, slowly nodded and took up a position at the side of the cart.

Jared walked quickly to the inn. Damn the child, he thought, why does she always answer with the shake of her head, you would think she was addle brained. Either way that wasn't to think about now when he could hear the sounds of laughter and company from the other side of the door.

Grace remained where she had been told to wait and looked at the scene around her. The days business of the market was winding down. The traders were packing up their goods with various degrees of satisfaction and sharing talk of the day. Grace looked down the long main street of the town and out towards the countryside that lay beyond.

Although she knew that she had never been to Honiton before, she somehow felt a strange sense of recognition about the place. It was the largest town she had ever seen, full of so many people all busying themselves with their own work...still buying and selling...talking and shouting, even now at the close of the day's trading. Everywhere she looked there were interesting things to see. There were large houses all down the wide main street where the market had taken place and where all the stalls were now beginning to be closed up and taken down. She wondered why if it was all so new to her, did she have this feeling. Perhaps she had dreamed it from talk she may have heard back in the village. She tried to think or remember but nothing came to her mind that could explain what she felt. No matter. The day had been interesting with so many new sights and sounds and even her uncle had not taken too much attention of her and now she was beginning to feel hungry, tired and wanting only to make the journey back home to the village.

Suddenly as she looked around, something caught her eye. Across the wide street and huddled up against a wall was a figure that when she looked more closely seemed to be an old woman dressed in rags and leaning on a staff with a hood covering her head. It appeared that the person was staring directly at her, and indeed was holding out something in her outstretched arm. She looked round to see if there were perhaps someone else who the old woman was gesturing to but there could be no mistake, it was her.
 She started towards the other side of the marketplace and then half way across stopped as she remembered her uncle's words and warning, she had felt his belt too many times not to know that it had been no idle threat.
She turned back towards her place by the side of the

cart but felt an overwhelming feeling willing her to turn again. She did and the old woman was still there in the same position with her arm out but now Grace could see what it was that was in her hand. It was a small doll and it was as if it were being offered to her.

She summoned all of her courage and ran across to where the old woman waited. As she drew close, she could see that the reason for the staff was that the woman was misshapen and deformed. She stopped again, now looking up at the face within the hood, which, when the woman slowly and seemingly with pain leaned down towards her, she could now see was as cruelly marked as her body. The voice though, when it came was surprisingly soft and gentle.
"A gift for you child "
Grace didn't answer but looked away from the face and back towards the doll.
"Does it not please you?"
In the few years of her life Grace had never been offered a gift. Slowly she nodded.
"Do you have many friends in the place from where you come?"
Grace shook her head.
"Then take it with my blessing, and may it be a true friend to you now and in the years that lie ahead."
Grace slowly reached out and let the doll be placed into her hands, at the same time fearfully looking back towards the inn, expecting to see her uncle angrily looking for her knowing she'd disobeyed him. She saw with relief that there was nothing but

the horse and cart.
Almost as if she could sense and even understand Grace's nervousness, the woman reached out a hand and touched her on the head.
"Go now child and be well."

Grace turned and rushed back across the street clutching the precious gift in her hand, knowing that even were Jared to come out and see her now, the doll would have been worth the punishment. She arrived back and took up her original position by the side of the cart. Some instinct made her realize that if her uncle were to see the doll there would be questions and so she carefully tucked it within the pocket of her apron. She suddenly remembered that in her hurry to get back she'd not thanked the old woman for the gift and so quickly glanced across the market to at least wave at her. She was gone, and though Grace looked around and down the street she could see no trace of her.

She touched her hand on her apron feeling the slight bulge of the doll. She wanted so much to take out and inspect this unexpected gift, but she somehow also knew that she wanted to keep all knowledge of it to herself. She was aware that her uncle could appear at any moment and she wanted nothing more than to begin the journey home so that she could look at the doll in secret when she was alone and no-one else could either see it, or take it away from her.

33.
The Inn.

There would have been no need for her to worry, for inside the inn and with his found "lucky money" Jared had celebrated his good fortune by drinking several tankards of the good strong local ale. He felt good. The warmth and comfort of his surroundings only brought home to him how little he felt like climbing back into his cart and returning to his small home and sour wife.
All the other men seemed to be happy and at ease. Why wasn't his life more like this? They were all laughing and talking, full of good cheer and fellowship, seemingly without a care in the world.

Across the crowded and noisy room he noticed one of the women who was talking to the innkeeper. She had long dark hair and seemed to have an easy manner and a ready laugh at whatever was being said to her. She turned her gaze away from the innkeeper and looked across to where Jared sat and met his look.
He quickly glanced away, embarrassed at the way she had seen him watching her. Something though drew his eyes back towards her and he could see that she was smiling now. She was smiling at him and he felt suddenly as if he were teen yeared again. He looked down but it was as if a force was drawing his face upward. He looked up again and met the same smile but this time it seemed as if it had another message in it. He looked at her eyes which slowly turned upwards to the rooms above

and then with a mixture of shame that he had not understood before and the desire that he felt within him he slowly nodded. The woman rose and walked up the stairs in the corner of the room. Jared fingered the coins left in the purse he had found, downed the last of his ale and followed her.

Outside the sky had darkened and a drizzling cold rain started to fall. Grace began to worry. It seemed that her uncle had been inside the inn for so long. Surely they needed to be making a start on their return journey and perhaps if she just moved a little closer out of the rain and inside the door he might catch a glimpse of her and remember that they needed to leave. She was torn between the fear of his anger and the misery of remaining out in the rain with the time passing and the journey home still to be made.

At that moment the door was pushed open and she expectantly looked hoping to see her uncle emerge but felt a bitter rush of disappointment when two men came staggering out, one holding up the other and helping him a few paces into the square where the man sank to his knees by the side of the cart and vomited on to the ground. She tried not to look or draw any attention to herself and edged closer into the still open doorway through which she was able to see into the inn. Just another few steps and she would surely be able to see her uncle and she could tell him about the men outside. She knew he would be pleased that she had thought about the safety of their horse and cart.

Her hand touched at the shape of the doll within her pocket. In some strange way, just the knowledge it was there and that it was hers seemed to give her courage. She took a deep breath, and in another couple of steps she was inside the inn enveloped by the smoky warmth, the bustle and the noise. She looked around desperately seeking a glimpse of her uncle. A woman bearing a tray and tankards set it down at a table next to her where three men were noisily drinking and laughing. She looked down at Grace
"And what can I be getting for you?
"I'm looking for my uncle" answered Grace quietly. The woman looked round the inn replying, "Well you'd best be finding him then." and moved away towards another table.

Grace looked round and towards all the dark corners of the inn although she still could not see her uncle. The men at the table next to her had gone back to their drinking. Grace was suddenly seized with a panic that she had been left and that she was alone in this busy and noisy place surrounded by strangers. She looked up at the men and tugged at the sleeve of the one nearest to her. He looked down seeming angry at being disturbed.
"Sir...have you seen my uncle? he is not here"
"How should I know your uncle girl " he answered roughly shaking off her hand from his sleeve " It's his business to look after you…my business is to sit here and drink my ale in peace."
Grace felt herself close to tears and then a thought

came, "Is there perhaps another room where he might be?"
All of a sudden it seemed that the man's anger had changed to amusement.
He turned to his companions, "Do you hear that. She wants to know if there's another room." at which the other men too began to laugh. He leaned down towards Grace and placing his hands on her shoulders turned her round towards where she now saw a narrow stairway in the furthest corner. "Take the stairs girl and then you'll find another room."

Grace moved away from the table and crossed the room to the stairway. At the bottom she hesitated and thought of simply returning outside and waiting no matter how long it would be. Somehow, although this seemed to be a better choice than risking her uncle's anger, she found herself climbing the steps to the top where she found herself on a landing at the end of which there was a door. She moved closer and hesitated wondering whether to knock or just quietly call out.
She heard sounds coming from the other side. They were harsh and angry…perhaps her uncle was inside the room and had become involved in an argument or even perhaps needed her help.

She opened the door and stepped inside. The room was small and as dark as the one downstairs. There seemed to be nothing in it except a small bed where to her sudden horror she saw her uncle fighting with a woman. They were locked together with her uncle grunting and moaning. Her dress had been pulled up and as he repeatedly pushed against her, the woman was gasping, moving her head from side to side and calling out words Grace did not understand.

Suddenly the woman looked towards the door and seeing Grace standing there let out a small cry. Her uncle too now looked up, the expression on his face unlike any that she had ever known. As Grace stood frozen in the doorway, he jumped up and pulling at his breeches which she now saw had been lowered rushed over to where she stood and fetched her a blow across the head that sent her spinning against the wall. She fell to the floor from where he grabbed at her hair dragging her to her feet again and slapped her across her face. Whatever it was that had been happening she knew that this would be worse that any beating she had ever had. She had never seen him angered like this. Surely he would let her explain…she opened her mouth to speak but before she could find any words he had brought the back of his hand down across her face again.

"Enough…you'll kill the child " It was the woman who had now risen and was shouting at him, seizing his arm before another blow could be landed.

He released his hold on Grace and turning to the woman roughly pushed her away. "And what would that be to you. What would a whore know of anything other than how to fuck?"

Pausing only to pull up and fasten his breeches, Jared dragged Grace out of the room and down the stairs. He rushed through the room and past the table where the man who Grace had asked about her uncle and his companions were looking towards them and laughing. Once outside, Jared gave her another blow to the back of her head and grabbing her by the hair pulled her over to the cart where he roughly lifted her up and threw her into the back. He hurriedly unhitched it from the post and mounting to the seat and cracking his whip drove as fast as possible away from the inn and from the town.

34
Remember.

Grace lay huddled in the back of the cart. Her head was throbbing from the blows she had received, and she felt sick with fear, but what was more scaring was that her uncle's anger had now become silence. They rode out of Honiton with the sky beginning to darken in rain that was now steadily falling.
Her fear grew as it seemed that they were not going back on the same road on which they had come. She was still dazed by what she had seen and what had happened, and she wondered where she was being taken.
After a while and with the town far behind them the cart began to move upwards on a narrow track. She sat up and could see that they were ascending towards the crest of a barren hill topped by a single tree.
She was overcome by a sudden panic at the thought that Jared meant to abandon her. She lay back down in the cart and though her head still ached from the blows she'd received; it was now the icy fear that ran through her that was more insistent. She moved her hand inside the pocket of her apron and touched the doll. A strange sense of comfort, and even warmth seemed to spread from her fingertips throughout her body, bringing a momentary calm.

The cart finally came to a halt with a jolt and she lay still. She closed her eyes. Above the sound of the raw wind, the rain and the harsh crowing of birds there was something else…almost a creaking scraping noise.

"Get up " The voice of her uncle seemed to have no anger in it but had a coldness that now seemed worse. She opened her eyes, sat up and felt herself roughly lifted onto the seat next to him. They were on the top of the hill across whose now fading light and the mist of the rain, she could see the countryside spread out below them.

Jared grabbed at her hair and turned her face away from where she had been looking. "There girl" he said pointing now at the lone tree by which he had halted the cart. She looked and felt her stomach turn over. What she'd thought was a tree was in fact a gallows, from which a black metal cage hung swaying in the wind, its bars just wide enough to allow access to the birds that were hungrily pecking at a body that was held inside. She could not contain all the pain and fear any longer and she bent over the side of the cart and vomited. When she had finished, her uncle straightened her up again and forced her face back towards the awful sight hanging there just a few feet above her. It was impossible to see what the thing before her had been in life… a man or a woman. All that was now left to see was a vision of such horror that she knew the sight would remain with her forever.

She tried to look away, but Jared tightened his grip on her hair and held her head towards the awful sight.

He spat out the words "If you ever tell of what you've seen today, then this is where I'll see you taken. You'll hang here as food for these birds, and you will be damned. Do you understand what I am saying?" he released his hold and took his hands from her head. Grace slowly nodded.

"Say it girl…say the words"

"Yes. I understand"

"Then look again. Look one more time and remember."

She looked back up at what had once been a person...a life that was now just a rotting carcass in a cage.

"I will remember."

It was dark by the time they returned to the village. Inside the cottage Anne had been making ready to serve the evening meal when Jared came inside followed by Grace.

"And was it a good day's business? "she asked sharply.

"It were no better nor worse than usual" answered Jared sullenly.

Anne looked past him to Grace and her expression clouded over as she noticed the bruises on Martha's face. "Come here into the light" she said, "What happened to you ?"

"The stupid girl tripped over and banged herself against a post by the side of the…"

"I asked her…not you" Anne interrupted him. She moved closer to Grace, bent down towards her and examined the marks. "You tell me girl how this happened."

Grace looked away from Anne's enquiring gaze to where Jared was standing and glaring at her.

"It was as he said. I fell over."

In a momentary flashback Anne's mind returned to her asking the same question all those years ago to Martha in this very same room…and receiving the same answer.

She turned and looked at Jared.

"Well it were you wanted me to take her to the market with me. She were more trouble than help" he said sullenly and moved to the table where he sat down without another word.

Later that night Grace lay in her bed unable to lose herself in sleep. Over and over she whispered to herself the same words. "I will remember. I will remember." Each time she closed her eyes she saw that dreadful scene and heard her uncle's words. The cold of the night and the chill she had taken in the rain felt that they would be a part of her forever. This cold, this aching cold and yet... There was warmth, a small isolated feeling of a warmth that also somehow took away a part of the fear. She moved her hand towards its centre and touched the doll that had lain hidden since she had received it at the inn, at that place and time that now seemed a different life before the bewildering and terrible sights she had witnessed later that day.

Slowly she brought it out and held it close to her face. In the dark she tried to think what material it was made of. The body felt harder than the rag dolls she had seen other children play with and yet surely it was also softer than wood. It was dressed in a plain and long white gown. Its hair was short but what there was of it was black like her own. The face had a serious and, she thought, almost a sad expression. Nonetheless she felt a soothing comfort slowly spread through her entire body as she looked at it. From what had been the worst day of her life there was still this gift that she held. She brought it to her lips and softly whispered to it. "You are mine. You will always be my friend."

She wanted something more. Something to make this gift truly her own forever. She needed a name. She thought for a few moments and then it suddenly came to her.

"I shall call you...Hope" she whispered.

And though she had earlier thought it impossible, she slept.

35
Pieces.

1620.

And so it was. The doll was her friend, and her only friend. The other children of the village had always kept apart, never wanting to include her in their games, always looking at her in a strange way and whispering to each other as she walked by. She had grown used to their taunts and unkindness and learned to ignore the cruel names they called her. There had been a time when it had caused her sadness not to understand why it was so, but it had always been this way and she had grown to accept it.

It was now fully a year since that dreadful trip to market and though she had accompanied her uncle several times since then, he had never gone back into the inn but had started on the return journey as soon as the day's trading was finished. For her part and though thinking of her often, Grace had never seen the old woman again.

She had tried to keep the doll hidden as a separate and secret part of her life but a day had come when she was doing some housework and the doll slipped out of the pocket in her apron and had fallen to the floor. Before she could pick it up Anne had noticed it and holding out her hands demanded "Let me see that."

Grace felt a sense of sudden panic. Since the day she had been given it, the doll had never been seen or held by anyone else. She knew that she couldn't refuse and so she picked it up and handed it to Anne.

Anne turned the doll over and over in her hands and then said accusingly "Where did you get this?"

Grace found it hard to lie but knew that the truth would only bring more questions.

"When Uncle last took me to the market with him, I found it laying in the street."

Anne looked hard at her. "Well I'd not thought that he would have bought it for you. What did he say about it?"

Grace knew that this time there was no point to lying. She took a deep breath. "He doesn't know."

Anne gave a half smile. "It seems you understand your uncle well and know the pleasure it would give him to take it away from you."

Grace felt a knot in her stomach. "Please...please do not tell him. It is the only thing that I have of my own."

Anne held the doll for a few moments longer and then her expression softened. "Then you'd best keep it close." she said and handed the doll back to Grace.

…......................................

Though it was not so very far from the village, somehow this place had always seemed special to her. Since she had first discovered it and whenever she had been able to escape from the routine and chores of her everyday life she had tried to come here. She had come to know this place in all the seasons of the year, and it was now as a golden and glorious autumn was turning the colours of the trees, and the smell of wood smoke scented the air that she had walked there.

In this small clearing near the river surrounded by the ancient trees she always felt a sense of peace and contentment. Whenever she had felt the sharpness of Anne's tongue or the stinging of her uncle's belt, this place had somehow made it better. It had brought her back to that feeling within her that somehow one day in the future all these things would perhaps change and be different...better. She did not know how or when that time might come but as she sat holding the doll gently between her hands there was a sense at least of that possibility. Though she had not realized it at the time, the name she had given her doll on that terrible day had come to her almost without thinking. She brought it closer to her face and spoke softly to share that dream. " It will someday be good for us. We shall go far away from them all. I promise this to you. I promise it to us."

Suddenly she was startled by the sound of laughter coming from behind the trees. She quickly tried to hide the doll beneath her dress, but it was too late. A group of the village children had rushed out to stand in front of her. There were the two brothers Jack and Tom and three girls, Mary, Agnes and Joan. She knew them as the various children of Jared's friends and also knew them to be no kinder than their parents. In the village they stayed away from her but seeing them here she began to feel threatened. One of the children, Mary who had something wrong with her foot and who walked with a limp and who Grace knew to be one of the unkindest now pointed at her mockingly.

"Look at her" she shouted.

Now they were all looking at the doll she held.

"What's that ?" said Jack

"It's nothing…it's…"

"It's nothing," he repeated in a sneering voice. "If it's nothing you won't miss it if you give it to me." Grace tightened her grip on the doll and slowly started to move backwards, but there would be no escape. A few paces behind her was the bank leading down to the river which just a few moments before had seemed peaceful and soothing but now had become a wall preventing any escape.

"Get it from her Jack…take it" shouted Mary.

Though she knew it would do no good Grace tried to reason with them.

"Please…it's mine. Just let me go home."

"We will let you go home once you've given it here" said Jack starting to move threateningly towards her.

Grace took another couple of steps back as all of the children now began to come closer. She noticed Mary stoop down to the ground and pick up a stone.

"Witch daughter" called out Agnes.

The others took up the chant

"Witch daughter…Witch daughter…Witch daughter…"

And then the first stone hit her on her shoulder, followed by another which struck her on the cheek.

Grace retreated further backwards still clutching the doll. Now she felt truly afraid as she felt the sloping ground of the river bank beneath her feet, and still the children continued to advance and still the stones continued to be thrown. She lifted her hands to her face for protection and at that moment stumbled backwards over a tree root and slipped down the bank and into the river. The sudden coldness of the water sent a shock through her body and she grabbed at a shrub at the side at the same time dropping the doll.

In a moment Jack had darted forward and seized it from where it had fallen. He held it up triumphantly to the laughter and shouts of the others," Look what it be...the Witch daughter still plays with a doll and she do talk to it...perhaps she be simple as well as wicked like her mother" He threw it high in the air. As it came down, they all grasped at it pulling and tearing, throwing it between themselves

.
Grace had crawled out of the shallow river edge and up the bank again. She was soaked through and also was now aware of the pain on her cheek where the stone had caught her. She knew there was nothing she could do or say that would make them stop. She watched with her heart aching as it all continued. She saw them pluck at the doll and the pain she felt was as if they were tearing at her. She watched helplessly as Mary and Margaret each took hold of an arm and pulled in opposite directions, shrieking with laughter as the arms came apart in their hands.

And then the game was over. The doll lay scattered

in pieces on the ground with no parts of it left to tear and break.

"You can have it back now " taunted Mary laughing "Or at least...what be left of it."

Grace stood there in a dazed shock. There was nothing she could say. There was nothing she could do. It was finished.

There was no more fun to be had and the group laughingly turned their backs on her and began to walk away back towards the village.

Grace stood watching them as they all disappeared down the path and then when she was sure that they'd gone she slowly walked over to where they had left the ruined doll. She bent down and sadly began to pick up the pieces. She was soaking wet and when she put a hand to where the stone had hit her cheek, and which was now beginning to throb with pain she realized that it had cut her and she was bleeding.

None of it mattered...the cold, the wet and the pain, what mattered was what she saw laying on the ground around her. She suddenly dropped the pieces that she held wanting only to run away, to leave it all behind her, to leave what had been her special place and which she knew was now spoiled forever. She wondered why she had ever named the doll. It was if there was some cruel message in what had taken place. For her there was no hope.

She turned and took a few slow steps back along the path and then she stopped. She closed her eyes for a few moments and listened to the sounds around her. What had been a golden autumn afternoon now seemed to be turning. The wind became stronger and with it more of the leaves came blowing down from the trees. The sound of the river which when she had arrived had been flowing steadily but gently now became faster, somehow more urgent. She knew that she could not simply walk away from that place as if nothing had happened and so she turned back again and slowly began to pick up what remained of the doll.

Eventually she had collected all the pieces of what had been her greatest treasure, her only friend. She looked down at them in her hands and felt such an aching sense of loss that she was sure that never again in her life would she know happiness. She thought of casting the pieces into the river one by one and letting the flow take them far away to wherever it would, but even as they were, dirtied and broken she knew that would be wrong. She closed her eyes. She knew there was only one thing to do. Holding the pieces gently and almost reverently in her hands as if they were somehow an offering, she walked back to where she had been sitting before the others had come.
 She reached the old tree. She knelt down beside it and felt the earth, it was soft and yielding. She started to scoop handfuls of it away making a shallow hole. A grave. After a few minutes she had made a space into which she gently laid the broken pieces, noticing with a sudden shock as she handled them that they were stained with the blood that had come from her hands after she had touched her

cheek.
The final piece she laid to rest was the head of the doll. She saw the face that had become so much a part of her life. For the last time she looked at the sad expression and almost wondered if the doll had somehow always known that this was to be its fate. Leaning down, she softly kissed it. She thought of saying a prayer and yet felt that no matter how much she had loved it, God might be angry with her if she used holy words for a doll. She closed her eyes and from somewhere deep within her the words came. She half spoke them and yet there was also somehow a melody within them that became a gentle song as she brought them out.

"Rest be inside you. Sleep now in safety
Peace be around you. You will always be mine."

She covered the earth over the top and slowly began to stand up. As she did, she began to feel faint. She leaned against the tree to stop herself from falling. She closed her eyes and pressed her face against the tree until she felt a little better. As she opened them, she looked at the trunk where a little way above her head she noticed a design that seemed to be carved into the bark. She tried to think what it could mean. She reached up and then raised her hand towards it and gently let her finger trace the outlines of what she could now see were entwined letters within a heart shaped design. For a few brief moments she was entranced by the carving and wondered how it came to be there and then she looked down once again to where she had buried the broken pieces of her doll, turned away, and slowly began the walk back to the village. She knew that she would not be able to tell of what had happened and resigned herself to accepting the punishment she would surely receive for her sodden clothes and cut face.

36
The Power.

She lay awake. There had been sadness in her life and there had been pain. She remembered the body hanging in the gibbet…there had been fear. Yet what she felt now was such an aching emptiness that she felt she would never be able to sleep again. Without the doll she was on her own as she had always been before that day at the market when the old woman had gifted it to her.
There was a part of her that understood what the others had meant when they had been taunting her and ripping the doll to pieces. She knew that she was leaving the years of childhood behind her. She was aware of changes in her body as she saw them in the other girls of the village, but what they had not been able to know was how much more than a childish toy Hope had been to her. She had experienced emotions that she had never in her life felt for anything or anyone else. Though the face of the doll had always carried a serious and almost sad expression, yet whenever she looked at its face she felt comfort and happiness.

The following days passed as if in a dream. As she had expected, Anne had wanted to know why she was soaked and cut, and she had told of trying to gather some flowers by the river bank and slipping. For his part Jared had not cared for any explanations just being satisfied to see her in that state, though that had not stopped him from giving her a beating.

It was not something she meant or even wanted to do and yet she felt drawn back to the place where until that day she had always known such a sense of peace and happiness. She walked slowly towards the base of the tree and saw that the wind had blown a covering of reddened leaves against the base of the trunk. The strangest thing was that rather than sadness she felt somehow a calmness. She paused for a moment hearing a sound above her. Looking upwards through the now almost bare branches of the tree she saw a single bird circling high above her.

She sat down beside the small mound of earth that she had dug days before, brushed away the leaves and gently placed her hand on it. She closed her eyes and listened to the sound of the wind through the treetops. The breeze held a chill within it, a forewarning of the winter that was soon to come, but Grace was aware of a warmth inside her. It slowly spread throughout her body almost as if she were warming her hands in front of the fire.

No…not her hands. It was coming from the one hand she had laid on the ground. She opened her eyes and looked down to where her fingers had almost unknowingly inched into the earth.

And the earth was slowly but surely moving.

Her first reaction was neither fear or shock but a sense of amazed wonder. She drew her hand away and stared at the place. There was nothing. It had been her imagination and longing that had caused what she thought she had seen and felt. Gently, lovingly she replaced her hand on the earth and again there was warmth…and again…there was movement!

Without waiting, without thinking she began to scratch and claw at the small grave she had made. A few frantic moments and she had taken away the earth that had covered the doll and her fingers reached down and clutched at the pieces and brought them to the surface.

And there were no pieces...The doll was whole. It was as it had been before. Its gown was dirty and still carried the bloodstains that had come from Grace's cut cheek. It still had the same rather sad expression. Except...Unbelievably... Its black hair had grown and was even the same length as that of the girl who now lovingly cradled the doll between her hands.

And in that moment Grace knew that she had the power.

She did not understand what it was or where it had come from, what it could do or how it could be used, only that it existed and was within her, and was now a part of her. For a few minutes she felt unable to move or to comprehend anything beyond that thought and though she could not explain or understand it, somehow, she felt different.

She carefully put Hope beneath her shawl feeling the warmth that somehow was coming from it spreading throughout her entire body and began to walk back towards the village in a kind of daze. It was as if time had either stopped or just begun to move in a different way. Had she been gone minutes or was it hours…she hoped not for surely then she would have to face the harshness of Anne's tongue or the rough anger of her uncle.

Her fears grew as she walked towards the cottage and she saw Jared outside looking down the lane towards her. She began to hurry and break into a run and then a strange feeling inside her made her stop and continue at a walking pace though she was already close enough to see the anger in his face, and how his hands were already unbuckling the belt that she knew would soon be used on her.

"Where have you been? " he shouted "Do you not know there are jobs to be done. I'll learn you not to…"

And then he stopped. He looked into her eyes in a way she could not remember him ever having done before…and she returned his look, now seeing in his eyes something she had never seen before. Was it pity or compassion, had he relented about giving her a beating…surely not, for he had never done in the past…what then? Before she had time to speak or offer any excuses for her absence he had turned away and walked back inside, where, having entered herself, she found him sitting by the fire silently staring into the flames as if they held some sort of answer to an unspoken question.

37
The first week

March 1621.

The year had turned. The early days of Spring were surely coming, though by the evening the air still held the chill of winter. For the most part the villagers stayed in their cottages by the fire and went early to bed though for some, the warmth and company of the inn offered more than they could find at home. And it was from the tavern, late at night with a belly full of ale and no more coin to spend that Edward stumbled out and began to walk back towards his cottage at the other end of the village.

Though the night was crisp and cold the sky was clear, and star filled. His mind felt fuddled and thick with all the ale that he'd drunk and so when after a few minutes he realized that he had walked the wrong way and in fact was going out of the village and towards the woods he could not help but laugh at himself as he turned and began to retrace his steps. A few more minutes and he stopped again, this time in bewilderment and some anger as he saw that rather than going back towards the inn, he had in fact walked further into the woods.
 He cursed the ale that he'd drunk, now beginning to feel sour in his stomach and turned again back towards the village. The warmth of the inn had now left him, and the cold of the night had begun to bite. Another few minutes and he would be back

there…perhaps even have another quick mug of ale to warm him again if someone might buy it for him. He stopped again. This time a sense of unease, even fear coming over him as he realized that not only was he not going in the direction of the inn and the village, but though he knew he could only be a few minutes away, and though he had lived here all his life…*he did not know where he was.*

"Are you lost?"

The voice came out of nowhere. He turned and then turned again, and in the moonlight, moving out from behind a tree and now standing a few feet away he saw a figure covered by a cloak and a hood. It seemed bent and crippled and was leaning for support against the tree.

"Who are you" he answered…

"Are you lost…Edward?"

At first, hearing his name he felt reassured. It was just one of the old women from the village, who would no doubt spend the next day gossiping with the other old crones about how she'd found him drunkenly wandering in the woods

As he moved closer, and by the light of the moon it seemed to Edward that there was something familiar about her.

"Do I know you?" he asked nervously.

"And where should you know me from." she answered.

He took another step towards her "Take your hood down and let me see your face."

She stepped back. "And why would you want to do that. I am no beauty."

There was something about this old crippled woman

that began to give him a feeling of unease. Beneath the cloak, beneath the hood there was something else…and now that she had spoken again, he realized that it was not the voice of an old woman. There was a part of him that wanted just to turn away and leave, but there was another part that wanted to know…needed to know.

"I said let me see your face or else…"

"Or else what?" the voice answered but with no trace of fear in it as if instead giving a challenge and then without waiting for Edward to make any reply the woman raised both her hands to the sides of her hood and slowly drew it back. Edward looked at her scarred and twisted face and then at the blackness of her hair which seemed almost to glow in the moonlight and realized that it was her injuries that at first had made him think of her as old. As he looked, the years fell away from his memory and he was again standing on a cliff top at Branscombe watching as a young girl handed her baby to her brother before falling to her death.

There was an icy coldness that now came over him and filled his entire being unlike anything he had ever known.

"You!" he gasped "It cannot be you…I saw you go over the edge."

There was a moments silence before the answer came.

"Do you know what you saw…or was it what your eyes wanted to see."

"I...I saw you. Jared told us. You were feared of the Witchfinder and jumped."

"Is that what he told you " she paused "And is that what you believed or wanted to believe ."

Edward suddenly wanted nothing more than to rush back to the village and tell the news of who had returned...but which was the way back? Everything around him felt different and somehow transformed. He thought it did not matter as long as he got away from this place. He turned and began to run away, but after just a few steps he felt as if his legs would not obey him. They felt heavy and cumbersome as if he were walking through mud...or even snow! He had a sudden flashback to how he and the others had trudged through the snow when they had been pursuing Martha all those years ago. Now it was him who felt threatened and wanted only to escape. He fell to the ground and fearfully looked back towards where he had left her.

Nothing!... She was gone.

He knew he had to get back to the village to tell them and to warn them. He began to get up and then realized with a growing fear, that he could not stand. All his limbs now felt leaden and useless almost as if he were trapped and held captive within a spider's web. He looked upwards beyond the treetops to where the stars seemed to be shining brighter than ever…brighter than was possible. And then, shutting out the stars came a dark shadow. For the briefest moment he was relieved. It was not the one he had just seen or thought he had seen. He could not make it out until it was inches away from his face and his mind began to crumble as the full horror of what he was looking at took away the stars forever.

38
Found.

In the chill of the following morning Edward's wife Catherine walked to the inn, her anger rising with every step. Once again, she knew that he had been spending what small coin they had drinking himself senseless. He was probably still curled up near the now cold embers of the fire...well she would soon wake him up. She reached the inn and banged on the door. After a few moments James the innkeeper slowly opened up. He looked hard at Catherine "Why all the noise at this hour?"
"Is that worthless husband of mine lying drunk again on your floor "she demanded angrily. "If he be then you'd best drag him out."
"He's not here mistress, the last I seen of him were when he staggered out of the door last night."
"And were he drunk as usual" questioned Catherine. James laughed "And is it my namesake good King James that sits on the throne?"
Catherine gave a snort, turned away and began to walk towards Ralph's cottage further down the lane. Perhaps as other times before Edward had gone there to sleep it off rather than return home to face his wife's anger.

By mid-day Catherine had tried all of Edward's friends and other places in the village where he might be found and with each negative answer slowly but surely her anger was turning to unease and then to fear. Surely, she was no harder and sharp tongued that the other wives in the village, but what if Edward had decided to leave her. Yes there had been times when they had argued and he had threatened to go off to Exeter and seek a different life, but that was what all men said when angered, did they not?

Finally she went back to the inn where James was outside mending some barrels. He looked up as she approached. Her demeanor was very different from when he had seen her early that same morning. Now there was concern and worry on her face rather than anger.

"He is not to be found" she said beginning to sob. The innkeeper stopped what he was doing "And you have asked of him everywhere?"

She nodded "That I have."

"Go back to your home" he said. "I will call some others. And we will have a search outside the village."

"But why would he go"

James smiled comfortingly at her. "That be something you can ask him when he come back with us." he gave a little chuckle " That be when you've finished with him."

Catherine softened and gave a sad smile. "That I will...and thank you." she said as she turned and began to walk away.

Within the hour James had gathered a few of the village men including Jared, Peter, Will, Thomas and Ralph who were happy to leave whatever work or tasks they had been at. Together they set off to search the local area. Their mood was not too serious as they walked the paths that led away from Clanton, surely this was a change from the daily

routines and would make a good tale that night at the inn.
As the time passed with no sight of Edward, the feeling among the searchers changed and the thought that he might have indeed left his home and wife became more and more likely. They reached the woods that lay a short way from the village. James suggested that they might separate to raise their chances and was just trying to decide who would go which way when Peter, who had walked off a few paces to relieve himself suddenly shouted out. "He's there…the drunken old fool" and pointed a few feet away in the undergrowth to where Edward lay on his back sleeping the drink off.
The other men saw where he lay and moved towards him joking about the scolding he would be in for from Catherine when they had helped carry him home.

Not just the joking, but any speech ended when they reached Edward and realized they were looking at death…and not just death but something else as well. Edward lay on his back, his face frozen into a mask of pure horror.
The blood that had come from his slit throat, now congealed around his neck like a macabre scarf. And even this was not the worst of it as the men stared down to where Edward's eyes had been and which were now only empty blackened sockets, each sprouting a shining black feather.

…..
In the village there was talk of nothing else. Everyone seemed to have their own ideas on Edward's murder, but when all the talk had been

done with, the only thing that could be agreed on was that nobody really knew. No-one had seen him since he'd left the inn. There had been no arguments. He had spent what coin he had till his purse was empty and even if somehow there had been a motive to have had his throat cut, why would his eyes have been taken? and even beyond that savagery…the feathers… why the feathers?

A week passed with the village remaining stunned by the event. The Coroner was summoned and came from Exeter. A court was convened in the meeting house at which he heard all the available evidence and spoke to different people, to those who had seen Edward drinking in the inn, and to those who had found the body. He dismissed any theories and speculation regarding the strange mutilations that had been carried out on the deceased.

The basic truth was that he had died from having his throat cut and anything else was, however horrific, incidental to that fact. He had his clerk take down notes for the record and then directed the coroner's jury of assembled villagers to the only possible verdict, that of willful murder by person or persons unknown.
The coroner and his clerk stayed the night at the inn and then left the following morning, wondering about these country people with their wild ideas and superstitions. It was just another murder the like of which happened in his own city of Exeter regularly. Men argued and they fought. They settled old scores, they stole, and sometimes they killed each other. This was surely just another such event.

39
The second week

The village was still in a state of shock and also fear after Edward's violent death, but now that the coroner had given his verdict and returned to Exeter, that, at least officially, was all there was to be done. It was now time to arrange the burial after which it was hoped the village could move on with their lives and hopefully put this single awful event behind them. It was decided that the funeral would be held on the following Friday and so on Wednesday morning, Ralph, as the Tower captain of the bell ringers made his way to the church in order to put a damper on the single bell that would sound out its mournful and muffled toll on the day of Edward's burial.

The church was empty as he stepped inside. He presumed that Henry Wilkin was as usual in the vestry penning another of his ever long, and Ralph thought, tedious sermons.
He slowly climbed the steep and winding steps that led to the bell chamber. At the top he paused to catch his breath and felt in his pocket for the leather pouch that he would use to tie around the clapper. He looked around for the ladder that usually was stored in the corner and which he needed to be able to reach the bell. He stopped and stood still.
It was as if the very quality of the air in the tower had changed and a sudden and overwhelming feeling of nausea came over him. He moved over to the slits in the wall and tried to breath in some fresh

air. He turned towards the top of the steps that would lead him back down but now as well as the nausea there was a dizziness that made the descent down the narrow steps seem too daunting until the feeling would pass.

Of course, he suddenly thought. Not down... but up. He looked towards the other steps that would lead to the outside and the top of the tower and pure fresh air. He quickly mounted the few steps, opened the door, and stepped out onto the tower top taking deep gulping breaths. Little by little the symptoms of his nauseous attack faded, and he felt his head begin to clear. It had been nothing, he told himself. He had not been sleeping well, if at all, since the discovery of Edward's mutilated body. There were so many questions and no answers. He knew that time would lessen the shock and that life would resume as before, but until that time came it was only to be expected that he would feel this way.

He moved over and stood at the edge of the tower looking out across the village to the rolling countryside he had known all his life. Spring was settling across the land. Despite the chill in the air the day was bright and clear. He swept his eyes around the view. There were the woods where they had found Edward with his throat cut. He shuddered and looked in the other direction where in the distance he could see the shimmer of the morning sunlight on the sea.
He looked towards where the hills rose and became cliffs, the cliffs where Martha had jumped to her

death. For some strange reason his mind seemed to go back to that day. He had not remembered it for so long. What must it be he thought… eleven... twelve year or more, and now the baby they had carried back to the village with them had grown to be so like the mother, and not just in her looks but also her strange ways. Lately he had even had the feeling that Jared was a little feared of her.

He looked up at the sun from which a movement came towards the tower. As it got closer, he now saw it to be a bird of some sort. It circled the tower, now swooping low and then climbing upwards before winging away across the village. He gave an involuntary shudder as he immediately thought of how Edward had been found. Trying to erase that awful memory and now feeling a little better for the fresh air he'd breathed, he turned back towards the door to do what he had come for and to muffle the bell. As his hand grasped the door handle, he heard something behind him. He turned at the sudden sound to see…to see what? Was it a figure, or a shadow? The sun was in his eyes and he raised a hand to shield them, though strangely even having done this, the sun seemed brighter and yet the figure seemed darker.

He felt a wave of fear and panic go through him and tried to open the door that led back inside the tower. The handle seemed to be stuck and would not move. He opened his mouth to speak…to call for help even though he knew he was alone, and yet found himself unable to form any words. He turned around and stood with his back pressed against the door. It was impossible. He was alone, and yet standing just a few feet away on the top of the tower was someone else. The figure shrouded in a black cloak neither spoke nor made any sound and yet moved slowly towards him.

He edged away from the door and moved to the side of the tower. He knew he must go forward, confront the figure, push past it and get back to the door at the top of the stairwell and yet at the same time he felt himself almost in a trance like state and only able to move backwards and away from the thing that kept coming closer. He was aware now of the stone of the tower's edge pressing against his back. He must make a break now or he knew it would be too late, but somehow it was as if there was a strange force between him and the figure that prevented him moving in any other direction other than backwards.

Backwards…
As he tumbled over the edge, he felt it was as if he were falling to the ground below in slow motion. Which gave him time to know what had been his last sight.

There was only one witness. Old Alice, who had been in the churchyard laying flowers by the headstone of her long dead husband. She was aged and half blind and so could not entirely be relied upon for what she later said. Which was that looking up from where Ralph had fallen, she thought that she had seen a face staring down...but when further questioned she agreed that what she had seen might just have been a trick of the light.

...or perhaps a bird.

40
The Third week.

It was as if the very air was thick with fear. Surely Ralph falling to his death so soon after Edward's murder was like an omen or a curse that had descended on the village. Again the Coroner had to be summoned from Exeter and again there were questions, and as with Edward there were to be no answers. It was surely an accident pure and simple. Unlike Edward there had been no mutilation. Ralph's body was found where he had fallen, twisted and broken but no more than was to have been expected by the fall. As for the look on his dead face, that too seemed only natural when consideration was given to the terror he must surely have experienced in what he must have known were his final moments.

Edward's funeral had taken place, though without the muffled tolling of the bell, none of the other ringers wanting to enter the bell tower, some from respect and others from fear.
The verdict that the coroner had directed to be found was simply that Ralph had died by the misadventure of the fall from the tower. It was in every way unlike what had been the case with Edward, and that was an end to it.

A week later on the eve of Ralph's burial, Jared and Thomas sat in the corner of the inn by the fire. For a while they were silent just watching the flames as they crackled in the hearth. It was Thomas who finally broke the silence.

"Is it not strange for Edward and Ralph to have died so close together ?"

Jared thought for a moment. "It's just the time that be strange. The one death were an accident that could come to anyone and as for the other, for Edward, it were murder as the Coroner from Exeter did say."

"I know it were murder" replied Thomas "But why murder a man who had no money on him nor anything worth stealing?"

"Perhaps he met someone and fell into a fight." suggested Jared.

"If it were a fight, you know he carried no knife and yet whoever killed him did, so why would he not have just run?"

Jared made no answer, there being none to make and just continued staring into the fire.

"And one more thing" said Thomas "If it were a fight and the other man would have had a knife, would he not have been stabbed rather than had his throat cut?"

Jared seemed to think this through, seeing the sense in it, but then another question occurred to him.

"You may well be right, but fight or no fight, what troubles me is what happened to his eyes. Why those feathers, as if there was a meaning?"

With this unanswerable thought between them both men now became silent. After a few moments Jared raised his tankard. "Whatever the truth, whatever the meaning, here's to both Edward and Ralph and may they rest in peace."

Thomas nodded and raised his tankard. "To that I do

say Amen." Both men drained their tankards, slowly stood up and left the inn, each hoping for nothing more than a good night's sleep before the morrow.

41
Burial.

Some spring days have the sure promise of the summer to come in them, but the next day dawned gray and overcast, full only of the blustery March winds that blew around the Churchyard. By eleven o clock the service in the church was over and the congregation stood and made ready to move to the churchyard for the burial. There was a calm but accepting sorrow among the gathered villagers, but unlike the recent and dreadful murder of Edward, this was something they all could understand. A death by accident can come as easily to a man falling from his horse as from a church tower.

As the rough pine coffin was carried out of the church and towards the waiting grave, a sudden gust of wind blew some fallen leaves in a flurry across the graveyard. The coffin, carried by Jared, Thomas and two other villagers followed by Ralph's sobbing widow Judith with her daughter Mary limping beside her, came to a rest beside the freshly dug grave. It was slowly lowered from the shoulders of the bearers and laid on the two planks which supported it above the waiting grave. The ropes were laid under and around it and the assembled villagers grew silent as the planks were taken away and the coffin was slowly eased down towards its final resting place.
Henry Wilkin began to speak the words of internment.
"Forasmuch as it hath pleased Almighty God to take

unto himself the soul of our dear brother here departed; we therefore commit his body to the ground. Earth to earth, ashes to ashes, dust to dust, in sure and certain hope of the resurrection to eternal... "
He stopped in mid-sentence as there were gasps from the people around the graveside.
A sound...!

Was it a trick of the wind, which now seemed to be increasing in strength?
No… More than that. Something else. People looked to each other, they looked upwards to the branches of the trees and to the Church and its tower.
Was it a moaning…a sound of something in pain? There was a horrified silence now as everyone tried to listen and to understand what it was that they were hearing.
Again a sound, this time accompanied by a scratching and scraping…

From inside the coffin.

The silence now shattered by a piercing scream from Judith "He is alive! Oh Dear God…he lives" Willing and eager hands quickly brought the coffin back to the edge of the grave and tried to pull at the lid which had been nailed fast the previous night at Ralph's cottage. Old Giles the gravedigger who had been waiting a few feet away ready to lay the earth in the grave now stepped forward with his spade and tried to pry open the lid, which seemed only to budge an inch and then held fast.

One of the villagers ran back to the works shed which adjoined the church and returned with a piece of metal which he inserted in the small gap the shovel had made. The lid slowly began to rise as the nails gave way. People crowded forward to see whatever there was to be seen. The silence had ended, and it was if everyone was trying to talk at once and above them all was the voice of Henry Wilkin beseeching God for a miracle.

Then a stilled moment as the lid suddenly came loose and fell away to the side revealing Ralph's corpse, and far from being alive it was not only dead, but had become a thing of horror. The face, which the previous night had been cleansed and prepared for burial and had seemed at peace, was now frozen into a mask of pain and fear.

Worse though than any of this was the coal black raven that sat on Ralph's chest pecking at the bloodied empty sockets where his eyes had been.

At first no-one moved. The sight was beyond belief and beyond comprehension. It was as if a spell had been cast over the mourners from which none were able to break out and either speak or take any action. Suddenly the bird moved its wings and lifted out of the coffin and towards Jared who brought both arms across his face for protection and dropped to his knees. The bird crashed against his arms and then turned into the sky where it flew through the graveyard and towards the church tower from which Ralph had fallen to his death. It slowly circled the tower and then silently moved away across the village and towards the open countryside.

…..

There could be no doubt now. There was evil and witchcraft in their midst. In the days that followed, a change came to the village that was more than fear...much more. It was among them and in their every waking moment.
It was suspicion.

Villagers who had known each other all their lives now passed each other by with only a quick greeting and a nod of the head. Word of what had happened at the graveside had been sent to Exeter and this time the Justice and his clerk had ridden out to investigate. But investigate what? There had surely been no murder here. The man had died from an accident, and yet surely there had been a crime. Why had the body been desecrated? And how could anyone have put the raven inside? The casket had been sealed in front of several villagers. It had lain the night in the man's house with no-one but a grieving widow, her daughter and a couple of villagers to keep a vigil.

The Justice spoke to people, questioned them, and then still finally had to admit that there was no reasoning behind it all.
Perhaps someone had held a grudge against the dead man. Surely that would be the most simple and obvious answer, but how then to explain the sounds

that had made them want to open the coffin. Someone would know, of that he was certain, but he had neither the time nor the inclination to remain in the village and make further investigations. He would return to Exeter, make his report, and there the incident would end.

For those who had been at the burial and had witnessed what had taken place, what the Justice and his clerk were to report as an incident, would never end. As the raven had flown away, Ralph's widow Judith had collapsed into unconsciousness. His daughter Mary had started a screaming that seemed as if it might never stop. Thomas, still standing looking down at what lay in the coffin was sick. As for Jared, as sleepless nights and uneasy troubled days followed, it was not the defiled corpse of his friend that reached into his very being and twisted at his guts.
It was only the raven.

42
The fourth week

It somehow seemed almost overnight that although it was spring that was showing itself in the buds on the trees and hedges and the flowers that were sprouting through the earth, there was only winter that had settled in the heart of the village and all who lived there.
 When they did have need to venture out, people tried to be accompanied rather than be alone, and none more so than Jared. He and Thomas now seemed inseparable. They spent as much time as possible in each other's company, and in the evenings, they sat together in the inn always leaving at the same time and walking side by side back to their cottages, parting only when they had to finally go down different lanes.

It was in the early morning just over a week after the horror of Ralph's funeral. Jared had gone into the barn to feed the horse and had looked over to the cart. It was tilting on its side. He moved closer to examine it and saw that the wheel had been broken and was hanging off its axle. After the first moment of anger at yet more work that would need to be done to repair it he suddenly wondered how he'd not noticed it when he had put the cart into the barn. He cursed the thought of spending time in the cold barn rather than at the inn. He thought of leaving it till the next day then realized that he had to be up early to take some goods from Clanton to a village a few miles away and so like it or not he would have to get on with it.

He left the barn and quickly walked to Thomas's cottage. It was a two-man job and he knew that Thomas would be as glad of the company as he, especially if there was a jug or so of ale to speed the work.

Thomas for his part had been only too willing to get out of his cottage for a while, even if that meant doing some hard work, and so they both walked back to the barn, gathered the few tools needed for the repair and set to work.

Though the job itself was straightforward and Jared had done it many times before, for some reason it was not going well and though the barn itself was cold, both men were sweating. For the last hour they had worked silently and now felt that they had earned a rest. Jared went to the open barn door and called out for Grace. There was no immediate answer and he raised his voice to a rough shout. After a few moments she appeared, wiping her hands on a cloth.

"Where were you.?" he demanded angrily.

"I'm sorry. I was busy and I..."

"Damn you I don't care what you were at, now you are here go bring some ale for us and be quick about it."

Grace turned and went back to the cottage. Within a couple of minutes she returned empty handed.

"There is no ale there."

Jared's face reddened "Of course there is you stupid bitch. Do I have to go back and get it myself? There is a jug on the shelf."

"I found the jug, but it was empty." Grace replied quietly as if ignoring Jared's anger and insults. Jared reached in his pocket and taking out a purse drew a few coins which he then threw down at Grace's feet. "Then go to the inn and get it filled." Grace bent down and picked up the coins laying on the ground. Jared and Thomas agreed that this was as good a time as any to take a well-earned rest.

Thomas had brought a loaf of bread and some cheese with him which they shared out and began to eat. Perhaps after that and a drink of ale they would quickly finish the repair and then go to the inn. They both sat down with their backs against a bale of hay to wait for Grace's return.

Thomas looked towards where Grace had just left. "She do grow more like her mother by the day." Jared nodded. "She do that" he paused "An' in more ways than you know."
"What do you mean?" asked Thomas.
Jared seemed unsure or unable to put his feelings into words and was silent for a few moments before answering "It's the way she do look at me sometimes."
Thomas laughed "It sounds as if you be scared of her. Perhaps you need to use your belt more often." Jared made no immediate answer as he realized that he had not used his belt for a very long time, in fact ever since that time she had come running down the lane and then just slowed to a walk and looked into his eyes. Then he quietly said, "I think she might even have some of her mother's witch in her."

The two men were silent for a few moments each in their own way remembering Martha.

It was Thomas who broke the silence. "I heard tell that the witchfinder be at Wilminford. There be a case against the wife of a farmer who they say put the evil eye on a farm next to her husband's where all the sheep went sick and died and her husband's didn't."

"How do you know."

"There were a traveler who had passed through the village that I spoke with at the inn."

"And what happened to the wife?"

"Don't rightly know " replied Thomas "I 'spect we'll get to hear of it one way or another."

The minutes passed without the return of Grace. Jared felt the anger rising in him.

"Where is that bloody girl ?" he said.

"Perhap' she stopped to talk with someone." answered Thomas.

Jared gave a mocking laugh, "There'd be none in the village that would want to pass the time of day with her. She'd never had no friends...nor ever will. She be too strange."

Thomas stood up and walked towards the door where at that moment Grace reappeared carrying the ale. She offered the jug to Thomas who eagerly took several deep swallows.

"Leave some for me you greedy pig" called out Jared.

Thomas took another long swig and then passed the jug back to Grace who began to walk over to where Jared still sat waiting impatiently wiping his brow with the back of his hand. As she came near to him the horse, which until then had been standing quietly eating, suddenly started forward and with a loud neighing began to paw at the ground with its hoof. She stumbled and fell, dropping the jug whose remaining contents spilled onto the ground.

"You clumsy fool " shouted Jared " Go back and bring some more ale and next time be sure to offer it to me first."

Without a word Grace picked the jug up and rose to her feet and began to walk back towards the inn. Jared moodily stood up and went over to the horse to try and calm it down. Damned girl, he thought…not offering the ale to him before Thomas. Perhaps it was about time she felt my belt again, or bed without her supper, then she would…

"Jared. Help me"

He looked over to where Thomas as if in a slowed motion was sinking to his knees. Jared ran across and reached him as he fell sideways on the ground.

"What be wrong with you ?"

Thomas made no reply other than to groan and close his eyes. Jared moved him so that he lay on his back. Thomas's face was a mask of pain from which all the colour had drained giving him a waxy and ashen look.

"Speak man, what be wrong, are you sick?"

Jared grasped Thomas by the shoulders and slowly raised him into a sitting position laying against the cart.

Thomas had opened his eyes and seemed to be looking not at Jared but beyond him, and he saw that the expression on Thomas's face was no longer that of pain…but of fear. Instinctively Jared looked round but seeing nothing turned back to the man now opening his mouth and trying to speak though his voice seemed strained and tightened as if unseen hands were around his throat.

"Dear God…it cannot be."

"What do you mean…what cannot be?" asked Jared

"There. Beside you. Oh sweet Jesus. Can you not see?"

Jared immediately thought that Thomas had suffered some kind of seizure. To try and calm the delirious man, he stood and made a show of looking around before kneeling back down to Thomas and cradling his head in his arms "I swear it man. There is nothing. There be nobody but I"

Thomas's face was now covered with a sweaty sheen and his eyes had taken on a glazed look. As he opened his mouth to speak, a thin trickle of blood seeped out and ran down his chin.

"We did wrong." he gasped.

A sudden chill ran through Jared as he answered, "What do you speak of."

"You know what I speak of. Those years ago. What we did to the boy, and then after that, to your sister."

Jared became angrily defensive "We did nothing. My sister jumped to her death. You know that." he paused "And the boy...well we did what we did. We were younger then and..."

Thomas's eyes clouded over as if misted by a fog and his voice became fainter and yet more insistent.

"We are damned. We be bound for the fires of hell. They have taken Edward and Ralph, they come

now to take me…as they will surely come for you."
"What do you talk of" demanded Jared, now feeling scared "What do you think you see?"
Thomas tried to make an answer, but his mouth seemed to be filling with more blood that ran out of his cracked lips and down onto his chest. Jared knew that this was not something that could be explained or understood and was filled with fear and panic but could see that Thomas was trying to speak, perhaps even trying to answer his question. He asked again "What is it you see? What is there?" and leaned down with his ear close to Thomas's mouth out of which was now coming a terrible rasping breath which seemed to stop for a moment as Jared moved closer and heard the last words Thomas would ever speak.
"You will soon know"

Jared moved his head away in horror as a foul smell came from the open mouth of the dead man. He stumbled to his feet and fearfully looked around. It was all madness…what was happening? Of course there was no-one there, it had just been the delirium of a dying man. He looked back down at Thomas's body on the ground. Around the mouth were the now congealing stripes of dark blood but there was something else too.
 Jared leaned down by the side of the body and fighting back his fear and revulsion forced himself to look more closely at the bloodstained mouth out of which Thomas's last choking words had come. There seemed to be something else other than the blood. Jared forced himself to reach down and

touch whatever it was. He grasped it between his thumb and forefinger and gave a slight tug.

Though the day itself was cold enough, he felt an icy and numbing sensation within himself that spread though not just his entire body but also the depths of his mind as a gentle pulling drew forth a blood-soaked black feather from out of the dead man's mouth. He fell backwards and felt himself overwhelmed by fear as he heard footsteps behind him. He turned.

Grace stood silently a few feet away… a look he could not understand on her face and the refilled jug of ale held between her hands.

43
The Witchfinder

The panic and fear that now swept through the village covered every street and every house as if it were a blanket of plague. There were questions. So many questions. *What had the men eaten?*... the same food. They had shared the loaf of hard bread and the piece of cheese. *What had they drunk?*...the ale…but no! Only Thomas had drunk the ale from the first jug. At the inn there were more questions. James the innkeeper had drawn the ale out of the cask from which others had drunk with no harm. He had passed the jug to Grace.
Wait…
There had been an old crippled woman who had spoken to Grace and offered to help carry the jug saying it was heavy for the girl. Grace was questioned and yes there had been an old woman who had helped her to the door.
What did she look like?
Neither Grace nor any of those at the inn could really say. She had worn a hood that seemed to cover most of her face, but anyway why would there have been any interest in her at all had Thomas not died.
Questions with no answers…deaths with no meaning. Who would be next? What could be done to stop the horror?
Jared's mind suddenly cut through the nightmare of what he'd witnessed and remembered what Thomas had said about Wilminford only a couple of hours fast riding away.

They would call the Witchfinder.

George Weston offered to make the journey and set out by mid-day.
It was as if a spell had been cast over the village. People stayed within their houses. There was little or no work done and even the inn, usually full and bustling with life and conversation was empty.

As the afternoon lengthened and the expected return of George and the Witchfinder was imminent, some of the men of the village ventured out of their houses and began to gather outside the inn. There was a strange atmosphere among them as they waited for the Witchfinder to come. Their faces were sombre and there were muted exchanges between them of what would happen next. There was still bewilderment and fear, but also something else. It was almost a strange sense of excitement as if they were to be a part of a drama that would unfold to either an explanation of all that had taken place over the preceding month. Or else....and there were none who could give word or thought to what that or else might be.

"They come" suddenly called young Giles who had been watching the road that led into the village. The men all looked round to see George Weston on foot leading his horse which was limping and accompanied by two other men approaching. George and the two men still mounted came to a halt by the side of the group outside the inn. One of them was a stout man with a balding head and a rough and angry look to his pock marked face, made worse by a livid scar that ran from his forehead and down across his eye to his cheek. He surveyed the huddle of villagers with a look that seemed to be of scorn. His companion could hardly have been in more contrast. He sat upright in the saddle looking slowly around at his surroundings rather than the gathered men. He wore a wide brimmed black hat and a matching cloak. Though the most immediately striking thing about him was a full and snow-white beard. Now he too looked around at the waiting group though with a calm and inquisitive eye. After a moments silence he removed his hat revealing long straight hair that fell to his shoulders.

He leaned slightly forward and addressed them in a firm and clear voice.
"This man who rides with me is Mark Pring my assistant and I am John Norris. I hold the King's warrant as Witchfinder and am here to flush out the evil that has come among you and investigate the allegations that have been made." He paused to let the full weight of his official authority be understood. "But first of all we must pursue and capture this old woman of whom I have been told. Do any of you know which direction she may have taken?"
For a few moments the men spoke among themselves.
"Perhaps she be gone toward Wilminford." said young Giles.

"If she had taken that road, we would surely have met with her." answered Norris slowly and dismissively staring down at the youth who had spoken as if at a simpleton.

Another man suggested "She might be goin' to Honiton."

Norris seemed to give this answer some thought before replying.

"You say she was old and crippled and on foot so she cannot have travelled any real distance. We'll follow the Honiton road and see if we can pick up her trail." He paused "Who of you will join me?"

There seemed to be general consent, even an eagerness to be part of the hunt. Some said "aye" others nodded, one villager cautiously suggested that perhaps the Witchfinder might want a rest or even a mug of ale before leaving, but Norris's immediate and stern response was that the Devil and his helpers did not rest and neither would he, and so straight away Norris turned his horse towards the road and said "Follow me now…we are on God's own work."

44
Pursuit.

The group of men moved off after Norris and his assistant and set off in the direction of Honiton leaving George Weston behind to tend to the lame horse and to tell of how he had ridden like the wind to summon the Witchfinder. For their part, Norris and Pring set a steady pace to allow the men on foot to be able to keep up with them. After a couple of miles there was a sudden rush of excitement as a cloaked and hooded figure was seen up ahead, though it was slowly coming towards them. When they got closer, they saw that it was just an old man with a few sheep straggling along behind him. Norris and Pring spurred their horses and rode up to the shepherd.

"Have you seen anyone on the road the way you've come?" demanded Pring.

The old man seemed at first neither to understand the question nor be too willing to make an answer. Pring raised his voice, "What be wrong with you...answer us damn you."

The old shepherd thought for a moment and then slowly replied.

"Well...there were an old woman a way back an' a while ago."

Pring seemed ready to lose his temper, "You old fool. How far and when is what we need to know."

The old man seemed neither to notice nor care about Pring's tone of voice. He looked up at the men questioning him and then past them down the track to where the group of villagers were now coming closer "Well I don't rightly know of that but she were walking slow and with a limp so she don't be that far ahead as there be nowhere on this road afore Honiton."

Pring muttered a curse and turned his horse back towards the men on foot who were by now approaching. Norris leaned down and spoke to the old man in a far gentler manner than that of his assistant. "I thank you. The Lord will know and remember those who help us to do his work."

The late afternoon was drawing to a close and the daylight was beginning to fade. The group of men were starting to become weary with keeping up with the pace of the two horsemen. Norris came to a halt to allow them a few moments rest.

"Come on you men." he encouraged. " Mark what the shepherd had said. We are on the right path and surely we hunt an old woman who cannot be faster than us."

"But if she be a witch there be no telling of how she may be able to outspeed us." called Will Bullen one of the oldest men in the group who was starting to tire.

"Yes…that be true and also it grows dark soon." agreed Peter Mills. A few of the men murmured their assent. When they had all been back at the inn this had seemed like an adventure. Now the night was closing in the thought of pursuing a witch was rapidly becoming less so.

Norris shook his head sensing the lack of willingness that seemed to be coming over them. "If it grows dark for us…it grows dark for her. Let us go on."

He spurred his horse and began to ride along the track. The men summoned up their energies and followed.

Another hour passed and the evening was turning to night, but at least it was clear and cloudless and illuminated by a bright moon that was now shining down on them. Norris brought his horse to a halt and turned towards the villagers. "See you men. God himself is giving us this moonlight. He is guiding our work and willing us on."

His words seemed to encourage them and after a few minutes rest they set off again following the Witchfinder and his assistant. Another hour passed and the villagers' original enthusiasm was now being overtaken by their tiredness and they were now starting to wonder why they had agreed to come on what was obviously going to be a wasted mission. There were also mutterings among them wondering how the old crippled woman the shepherd had spoken of could have gone so far ahead.

Ahead of them was a long and steep hill. Norris, understanding that it could well prove to be the final straw told them all to wait as he rode on ahead. He urged his horse forward followed by Pring. The men all sat down and started talking among themselves hoping that the Witchfinder would call a halt to the search and give them leave to return to the village and their beds. What had seemed a good idea and an exciting change to their everyday lives just a few hours ago had now turned into an exhausting and probably wasted journey.

After a few minutes Norris and Pring reached the brow of the hill and reined in their horses. The night remained clear and the moonlight gave them a commanding view of the surrounding countryside.

Each of them scanned the land ahead of them. Suddenly Pring saw a movement in the distance. It was too far to be sure, but it seemed to be a lone traveler. "There...down there" he shouted pointing towards what he had seen. The Witchfinder followed the direction of Pring's outstretched arm. "You're right...call up the men." He looked back down the hill waving and calling out to the group still resting at the bottom of the hill. His calls went unheeded. He turned towards Pring "Ride back and get them...I'll go on ahead."

Pring set off back down the hill shouting at the villagers. Before he was half way there, he had been seen and the men were hurriedly getting to their feet, sensing that perhaps their quarry had not escaped and that there was still a chance of success. He turned his horse and followed where the Witchfinder had gone, soon cresting the hill and reaching his side as they both closed upon the traveller ahead.

…..

In a few minutes Norris and Pring had caught up with the lone figure. It had neither turned nor quickened its pace at the sound of the horses coming fast up behind. Norris reached its side and indeed saw that it was an old woman who had now stopped and was looking up at him. Norris looked down at her in the full moonlight. She did seem to answer the description that had been given in the village. She was old and obviously crippled. The Witchfinder leaned towards her. "Who are you Mistress and why do you travel alone along this road at this time?"

The woman made no answer but continued looking up at Norris.

It was Pring who spoke. "Per'aps she be deaf as well as crippled."

Norris grunted and raising his voice repeated his question. Again there was no answer.

The group of men from the village having come over the hill and caught up to where the two horsemen were waiting had begun to run down towards the Witchfinder and what they now could clearly see was a woman but then, as if by common and unspoken assent they came to a halt several feet away. The Witchfinder looked towards them and in an impatient voice called them closer. "Get here you men. Are you all afraid of a crippled old woman? Do any of you know her and can you tell if it was she that came to the inn and took the jug from the child?"

The men who still had remained several feet away from the woman slowly started to move a little closer. As they did so the light from the moon vanished as a sudden and single cloud passed across it. The darkness and the hood she was wearing made it difficult for anyone to be sure.

"You do ask her" one of the men called out "Do she say she were in the village and at the inn?"

"She says nothing " replied the witch finder " Since I rode to her side and stopped her, she has not spoken or answered anything that I have put to her."
"That show she do be guilty…otherwise she would speak her innocence." said Peter.
One man who seemed bolder than all the rest called out. "Let me see her." It was James the innkeeper who had spoken and who now stepped forward to look at the woman more closely. He stood silently in front of her for a couple of moments peering at the woman through the darkness of the night and the covering of her hood.

 Suddenly a wind sprang up and blew across the assembled group. As it did so the cloud passed away, the moon was uncovered, and it was as if a hundred candles had been lit illuminating the entire scene. James looked again in this new light. He gave a gasp and then quickly stepped back and crossed himself. He turned towards the other men and in a strained voice and through a throat constricted with fear called out "Jared...Jared…you must come and see."
Jared had been standing with the other men who were now all looking towards him waiting to see his response. He did not know why he was being singled out and felt an overwhelming fear. "I told you. I told all of you that there was no-one to be seen when Thomas died. If she were there…I did not see her."
The witch finder leaned forward in his saddle. "Come forward man" he commanded impatiently. " Remember...this is God's work that we do."

Everyone had turned towards Jared and he found himself being pushed towards where the Witchfinder sat on his horse and the hooded woman remained still and silent. He moved slowly closer trying to prepare himself for whatever had so terrified the innkeeper. He reached the side of the Witchfinder and put his hand out and gripped at the saddle to steady himself. He took a deep breath and looked into the darkened depths of the hood. The sound that slowly came from his mouth was barely human as the first dawning of shocked recognition was followed by a panic such as he had never known. It was as if his entire world, everything he knew, everything he understood was turned on its head.
"What do you see man?" demanded the Witchfinder…" Do you know this woman? Speak."

Jared tried to form the words, but it was as if any link between his mind and his voice had gone. The Witchfinder leaned down and grabbed Jared by the shoulder. "Damn you. Will you not speak…are you struck as dumb as her?" He released his hold on Jared and instead leaned down towards the woman pulling at her hood which fell back revealing her face. Jared had fallen to his knees and closed his eyes as if that action could erase what he had seen, but he could still hear the gasps of shock and horror as the other men had looked at the woman and seen past the tangled matted hair streaked with gray and the deep lines etched in her face from the painful years of existing within her crippled body. They had looked beyond this and remembered a young woman of the village.

A woman who was dead.

It was James the innkeeper who was the first to find his tongue and break the silence.
"She be Jared's sister Martha…and she be returned from the dead."
The Witchfinder looked again at the woman. "What do you mean, returned from the dead…this woman is very much alive."
"No your Honour" James said, "She fell to her death from Branscombe cliffs twelve year ago."
The Witch finder looked down at James, then at Jared, still on his knees and then at the other men, all of whom stood in a shocked silence. He steadied his horse which had started to seem unsettled and finally looked at the woman who stood silent and unmoving.
"There is indeed witchcraft here. Bind her…we return to the village."
Still no-one moved. The Witchfinder shouted angrily "Are none of you men…do I have to dismount and tie her myself?"
At this a couple of the men moved forward and took the rope that the Witchfinder handed down. The woman remained still and silent as they bound her hands and tied the end of the rope to Pring's saddle. With a sharp pull on the reins, Norris turned his horse and without another word started to lead the group and their captive back toward Clanton.

45.
Jared's request

When they finally reached the village it was now fully night time and the bright moon still shone down lighting the group as they came through the lanes and into the main square. People in the cottages started to come out into the street and the identity of the captive spread within moments. Some moved closer to see if it was true and others drew back inside, crossing themselves and bolting their doors.

The group reached the small lock up that stood by the side of the meeting house. Richard Watten the locksmith who also doubled as the towns gaoler was summoned. He breathlessly arrived a few minutes later and unlocked the cell. Norris remained on his horse as Pring dismounted, untied their captive from the rope that held her to his saddle and roughly pushed her inside.

Watten turned the key in the lock and made as if to leave. Pring held out his hand for the key. Watten looked questioningly to Norris who, asserting his authority just nodded. The key was then begrudgingly passed over and handed to Norris who then turned to the men who had accompanied him.

"We have done well this night. I thank you all. Return to your homes…there will be time tomorrow to question her. You will all come to witness her examination and hear whatever it is she may then say. Till then a good night to you. For myself, I am to the inn to celebrate this night's work with a tankard of ale."

The men turned, eager to get to their homes and tell of what had happened and of their part in the chase and capture. Only Jared, still unspeaking and in a total state of shock hesitated, not understanding what he had seen and not knowing what he would say to Anne. He stood silently for a few minutes until seeing that he was alone, and that he had nowhere else to go, he too turned away and slowly walked back to his home.

His mind was spinning. It was as if the worst nightmare was upon him with no chance of an awakening bringing relief. He turned the corner towards his cottage and suddenly stopped at the realization of what tomorrows questions might be…and worse…what answers might they bring forth. He turned in his tracks and purposefully walked towards the inn.

He opened the door and stepped inside. There were some here from the group who, like Norris, had decided to end the events of that night with a few drinks. James the innkeeper was loudly telling of how he alone had been man enough to confront the witch...for that is now what they were calling her. There was a hubbub of conversation that stopped as Jared crossed the threshold and entered. He looked around, not feeling able to meet the glances that had been directed at him.

John Norris and Mark Pring were seated at a table in the far corner of the inn. Jared cautiously approached them. The Witchfinder looked up from his tankard of ale at Jared now standing in front of him.

"What is it you want man ?"

"Have you spoken with her yet?" asked Jared.

"You know that I have not…you saw Pring place her in the cell" replied the Witch finder. He paused, narrowing his eyes as he looked Jared "And anyway…what is it to you? I have done a full day's work in catching her. I sleep here tonight and will question her in the morning, until then she can wait in the lock up."

Jared swallowed and said in a quiet voice "I would speak with her in private."

The Witchfinder looked at him as if trying to guess what could be gained from any such meeting.

"And why do you now think she will speak to you when the knowledge and fear of what I have it in my power to do has not loosed her tongue? "

"I mean...I mean only to try and help you in your work." replied Jared.

"And is it that you have lost the fear that you showed when we found her?" He paused and looked hard at Jared before continuing "Or do you perhaps have an even greater fear that makes you bold?"

Jared tried to control the emotions he felt as he answered. " Sir…It was the sudden shock that had come over me. I thought..." he paused for a moment "We all thought that she were dead…that she had chose to take her life because even then she were to be accused of witchcraft. Surely it can only be the proof of that witchcraft that can have saved her then."

The Witchfinder looked steadily at Jared for a few

moments. "Perhaps you are right…but why then did she not use her spells and craft to save herself whole? Why would she spend years crippled and disfigured? Why would she have returned to a place where she was known? Above all, why should she have held grievance against the three men who have been killed?"

Without either expecting or waiting for a response he continued slowly and menacingly. "You see there are many questions to be answered when I examine her tomorrow."

Questions…answers…Jared's mind was racing as he tried to think of all the possibilities the Witchfinder's examination might open up and bring to light. In desperation he made one last appeal "Sir, I only think that I might as a brother make her see the sense of speaking the truth to you and so spare you much time."

The Witchfinder was silent as he considered what Jared had said. He had all but finished his work in Wilminford and surely there could be no harm in a meeting between the man and his sister for a few minutes…and if that were indeed to save him wasted hours and help speed him on his way back to Exeter and the comforts of his home then why not. He looked again into Jared's face trying to read the expression he saw there. Was it still fear? Was it hope? What matter. If the brother could not bring the woman to co-operate and confess to any ill doing, then he and Mark would use other well tried methods which he knew from his experience would indeed bring results.

"Very well. Go to where she is held in the lock up and speak with her. Be sure to tell her how it will go with her if she does not speak open and true with me when she comes for the questioning in the morning." He turned to his assistant. "You go with him."

Pring was obviously unhappy at the thought of having to go out again rather than staying within the warmth and comfort of the inn. He looked at Norris but saw immediately by the look on his face that there was little or no point in arguing the matter. He grumpily rose to his feet, lifted his tankard and downed what was left of his ale. Taking the key that Norris held out towards him and fastening it to his belt he walked to the door, Jared following a few paces behind.

46
The Lock up.

They reached the lock up and for a moment Jared tried to fight back the feelings overwhelming him. He stood outside the cell trying to control himself. The idea of being alone with Martha after what had happened to Edward, Ralph and Thomas filled him with fear and yet he knew that he must talk with her before the Witchfinder examined her. He tried to think clearly. If it was just revenge, then why had she not killed him first? He thought for a few moments. Of course…it was her way of making him suffer more with the knowledge that his turn would come…and yet the others were dead. What was to now stop her from turning her witchcraft against him. The harsh voice of Mark Pring cut through his thoughts and hesitation.

"Well man, are you going to go in or stand out here all night? Her hands are tied so what harm can she do you."

Jared looked into the man's scarred, pock marked and leering face and made his decision "Open the door."

Pring took the key from his belt and inserted it into the lock. Pausing for a moment he looked at Jared and grinned, baring his blackened and broken teeth "As I said, her hands are tied…but who knows what she may be still able to do with her witchcraft."

Jared felt the anger rising within him mixing with the fear in the pit of his stomach "Open the damned door and shut your mouth."

Pring made a mocking bow and turning the key,

slowly opened the door.

As he stepped into the small cell lit only by the moonlight from outside the barred window, he strained his eyes to become accustomed to the darkness. He gave a sudden start as he heard the door slammed shut behind him and then the scraping sound of the key turning in the lock.
At first, he could not see her and was swept by an overwhelming fear that she had used her powers and simply flown out through the small opening of the window. He tried to bring his panic under control and was on the point of calling out to Pring when he saw her. She was laying like a bundle of rags on the floor, huddled into the furthest corner of the room and with the hood of her cloak pulled over her head. Staying with his back to the door he called out to the figure.
 " Martha…it is me…Jared."
There was no answer and he felt the fear that he had tried so hard to overcome rising in him again.
"It is me. Will you not answer?"

The figure in the corner moved and slowly rose to its feet letting the hood fall away. Martha looked straight at him and for the first time in twelve years he heard her voice. She spoke quietly.
"And what answer should I make…brother?"
Jared tried to keep his voice under control lest it betrayed his fear " Why did you come back? There is nothing for you here except certain punishment and death."
Martha looked directly at him "Are you so

certain…have I already been found guilty? You forget that I came back from death once before." she paused for a moment before continuing "And yes there is something…or should I say someone here for me ."

"You mean the child…you mean Grace?"

"You called her well for it is surely by God's own grace that she thrives rather than the life you give her."

"You know nothing of her life " Jared answered angrily.

"But there you are wrong." Martha said quietly, "I have watched her and seen her at different times since that dawn at the cliffs. I have been close even though you would not have seen me."

"You're lying. I would have known…others would have seen you."

"Do I not speak the truth? Do you remember a time on Honiton market day when you had been whoring and I watched as you dragged that child from the inn by her hair."

For a moment Jared was speechless. "You were there?" he whispered.

"I was there…and also at many other places and at other times. In your house when I had heard you take your belt to the child it was as if the blows were falling on me."

Jared's mind was in turmoil and confusion "Why have you waited till now to take revenge on us all…on Thomas…on Ralph and Edward?"

Martha took a step towards him and he suddenly felt his legs become weak as he fought back the urge to run from the cell.

"And is it revenge…or is it Justice?"
Jared felt sick. There were so many questions he wanted to put to her. How had she survived the fall over the cliffs? Where had she been all these years? Crippled as she was how had she managed to kill the others, and yet over and above all these there was the single most important one he had to ask. "What is it that you will tell them when they put the questions to you?"
Martha looked into Jared's eyes and smiled at him, a smile that filled him with a terrible fear. "What is there to tell? Perhaps of a brother who raped his sister…who took her baby from her and then pushed her to what you thought would be her certain death. Is that what there is to tell?" she stopped speaking and the strange smile left her face as she continued. "Or should I tell about a boy who vanished."
Jared fought back the panic he had begun to feel and sneered "Do you mean the boy who ran away once he knew you were with child?"
"You know who I mean and of what I speak and know."
"You can know nothing."
"Is that what you think brother" Martha closed her eyes and breathed deeply for a few moments. "I see water. I see a boy fighting the pain as it fills his body and takes away his young life." she paused and opened her eyes, "and I also hear."
"What do you hear witch…do you hear Satan's voices?"
"No…not Satan. Neither devils nor angels. I hear the voice of a dying drowning boy calling out my

name."

Jared realized that he had begun to tremble and that his hands were shaking. He closed his eyes and took a deep breath before speaking.

"If you say even one word of this when you are examined tomorrow, I promise you…the child will die."

Martha gave him a look that he could not understand... was it defiance…was it capitulation? There was total silence in the cell. Jared moved closer to her fighting back his fear as he looked into the face disfigured by the years of living with her physical pain "Do you understand?"

She looked deep into Jared's eyes "You would harm your own child?"

The speed of Jared's response answered any doubts that Martha might have had.

"I will do whatever I must. Besides… the child grows ever more like you. There is something not right about her."

Martha closed her eyes and raised her head upwards. There seemed to Jared something almost trance like about her as the words came softly and quietly as if she were hushing a baby to sleep with a lullaby .

"Though evil unto me was done. My silence now lasts unto the grave.
And even were I not the one, Then she who is, I die to save"

Jared suddenly felt as if the atmosphere in the room

had changed bringing an oppressive closeness that seemed to affect his breathing. He took a step backwards and then turning away from the now silent Martha, banged loudly on the door.
"I am done here. Let me out."
There was no response and Jared felt overcome with fear. He must have been mad to ask to be alone in the cell with Martha…and now what new witchcraft was this. Surely Pring would not have gone. He banged again on the door.
"Open the door damn you…open the door." he shouted.
He forced himself to look round and was horrified to see that Martha was smiling now and slowly moving towards him with arms that had been tied when he stepped into the cell, now open as if to embrace him…
Or capture him.
He screamed "Let me out. Open up."
As Martha came to within a few steps of where he stood, the door suddenly swung open and Jared rushed out to find Mark Pring doubled up with laughter as he closed the door again. Jared's fear overcame his furious anger and he ran out into the night.

…..

He reached home. He had been desperately trying to think of what he would say to Anne and how he would tell her, but as soon as he entered and saw her standing by the fireplace, he realized that she already knew.
"Where have you been?" she asked him accusingly.

"I…I went …I went to speak with her." Jared stammered.

Anne looked directly into his eyes "And what did she have to say? What did you have to say?"

Jared tried to think. Anne had somehow always known when he was lying to her, it had shown itself in a certain expression on her face, but he had no choice, whatever he said, it could not be the truth. "I asked her why she had come back, why she had…"

Anne cut him short "You're a fool, you always were. She can only have come back for Grace. Do you think she would have come back for you?"

Jared became bolder "I spoke with her. I saw her...she is a witch. She came back to kill the others Edward, Ralph and James."

Anne moved closer to Jared "And why would she have wanted to do that?" she paused "and if them, then why not you?"

"She is evil" Jared blurted out "She always was"

"Remember Jared…I also knew her" she stopped and with a questioning look on her face said, "Perhaps not as well as you did, and yes, she was strange…but evil?"

"She was evil I tell you." Jared said defensively.

Anne looked into Jared's eyes "If there were evil in this house perhaps it was not all hers."

Jared could not hold Anne's piercing stare and looked down. Anne continued speaking "Perhaps we shall find and hear the answers to all these questions on the morrow when she is to be examined."

Jared answered too quickly "No, she'll not say

anything."

Anne was silent for a moment. "And how can you be so sure of that?"

Jared quickly thought back to when Martha had been taken. "She would not make any answer to the questions that the Witchfinder put to her. From the moment we caught her to the time she was placed in the cell she would not speak."

"We shall see" replied Anne "I have heard tell that the Witchfinder can be very persuasive." She gave Jared a cold look. "Whatever the morrow brings, I am to bed. You sleep here by the fire."

47
The Hearing.

April 1621.

The day dawned like any other, and unlike any other. The village was buzzing with the news of what had happened the night before and of the identity of the old woman. There were some who could not understand why if the rumour was true and it was indeed Martha then why they should think her old. It was over twelve years since she had fallen from the cliffs and she had been but a young girl then.

There were others who knowingly said that it was the witchcraft and dealing with Satan that made even a young woman appear aged. There were some who remembered Martha and told that she had always seemed strange and others who remembered her as a kind and gentle girl, but those who thought like this did not talk of it. On one thing there was agreement. Everyone wanted to be at the examination to see and to hear whatever was to be disclosed, and to this end, the people of the village made their way towards the Meeting house, where the examination was to take place.

When everyone was settled, John Norris made his entrance. He glanced around the assembly gratified to see that what seemed to be the entire village had turned out to see him carry out his work. Without a word he strode to the platform that had been set up and on which there was a table and chair. He

mounted the platform, seated himself in the chair and placed the Bible that he had been carrying on the table. He swept his eyes over the expectant villagers all looking towards him. He let the tension of the occasion continue for a few moments and then his firm voice filled the air.
"Bring the prisoner forth."
The low murmur of conversations and anticipation that had filled the room suddenly stopped as the door opened, and Mark Pring entered holding Martha by the arm. There seemed to be a calmness to her that almost seemed to deny the danger of her situation. She looked neither left nor right but just kept her eyes straight ahead. They moved slowly through the room until they came to a stop just before the platform where John Norris sat silently waiting. Pring then released his grip on Martha's arm and moved slightly away so that she stood alone in front of Norris, who asked Pring.
"Who do you bring."
He called out in a loud voice "I bring Martha Carter to answer charges of witchcraft and of causing death to three men of this village."
The Witchfinder looked slowly around the room and then down to where Martha stood before him with her head bowed down. "What answer do you make to these charges?"
There was silence as everyone waited to hear Martha's voice. A few moments passed and then the question was put again "Mistress Martha, there have been three unexplained and violent deaths in this village. You are here charged with involvement in them. We are here to see the King's justice done and

to give you the chance to speak out in your own defence. Will you now make answer to these charges?"
Martha still made no response other than to raise her head and look directly up at the Witchfinder.

John Norris looked down at the woman below him. In his official role he had examined many other men and women on charges that they well knew could result in their deaths. He had seen many different reactions and expressions on their faces, fear, guilt, repentance and many others, but he knew that he had never been met with a look such as he was now receiving from this woman. He found it hard to put a name to it, and then in a sudden understanding it came to him. It was pity! But it was not for herself and her situation. Rather it strangely seemed that it was for him. As if he were the powerless captive who had no choice other than to act out a role. He felt the anger rising in him. Damn the woman. He had thought that the time he had allowed with her brother might have brought her to show some sense. Surely she knew what awaited her if she held to this stubborn silence.

He looked across to where Jared sat, searching his face for any clue, but could find nothing in the man's ashen and tight expression to answer him. Damn the brother as well, he thought angrily. Perhaps he should have met with him this morning to know what had passed between them the night before in the cell.

The Witchfinder looked from the people gathered in the room back to where Martha stood silently

looking up at him.
"I ask you once again…and I ask you for the final time. Will you answer the charges that have been laid against you?"

There was a hushed expectant silence as everyone looked towards Martha who now lowered her head but still remained silent. Norris tried to control the anger and frustration he felt at the stubborn and insolent refusal of the woman to speak. It challenged his position and his authority.
"If you will not make answer, then it can only be that you have something to hide, and I say to you that if you now refuse to speak with free will then we shall loosen your tongue by other means."
He paused waiting to see Martha's reaction. In his experience, any who had remained silent up until this point now spoke out either with lies, excuses or pleas. A few moments passed before Martha slowly looked up at the Witchfinder and met his gaze with an expression that had now changed to one of resignation, then breathed deeply and closed her eyes.
The Witchfinder's voice carried across the assembly. "Take her back. She must be put to the test."
The silence in the room now came to an end as Pring now moved to her side, roughly grabbed Martha by the arm and led her out of the Meeting house.
A murmur of excited chattering broke out which was silenced by the sudden sound of the Witchfinder's hand being brought down hard onto

the table. "We shall assemble here again tomorrow at noon when the charges shall again be put to the accused." He stood up quickly, knocking over his chair and stepped down from the platform. As he did so he stumbled and fell. A couple of the men who had been standing close by moved to help him to his feet, but he angrily waved them back, stood up and then looking only straight ahead, walked grim faced out of the room.

……....................................

That night there was a strange atmosphere that lay over the village like a blanket. In every home there were conversations about the events they had all witnessed earlier in the day. As the villagers sat around their fires, they all wondered and spoke about what the following day would bring. Some spoke out of interest and with measured words. Some spoke foolishly with fear and superstition. Some, who mourned for the men who had died, spoke with hatred and revenge. But above all that was being said, and piercing through the darkness of the night came the sound of Martha's screams. They seemed unending and chilled even the hearts of those who believed her a witch and so deserving of what was now being done to her.

In the house of Jared and Anne there was no talking. They both sat silently, each with their own thoughts. With every scream and each passing hour Jared prayed that whatever the Witchfinder found out would not incriminate him. He knew that Martha had believed in what he had threatened to ensure her silence, but Dear God...surely what Norris and

Pring were doing to her would make her forget any threats of his in order to make her suffering end.

Grace lay in her bed, wanting only the comfort of sleep, trying not to hear the terrible sounds of pain that filled the night. She had not been allowed at the hearing and did not fully understand what was taking place. She clutched tightly at the doll held to her chest as if somehow, as so many times in the past, it would bring her some comfort, but this time no comfort came. She wanted to know, wanted to ask her uncle and Anne about the event that was taking place in the village. At the same time, even though some suspicion and inner knowledge told her that it was in some way connected to them, yet she knew instinctively that she must not.

48
Raven.

The following morning the villagers once again gathered in the Meeting House and this time with an even greater sense of expectation than the day before. This time they knew they would hear Martha speak. They had all heard her screams and cries the night before and were sure that it would have been impossible for anyone to hold to the obstinate and willful silence she had shown then.

As on the previous day John Norris entered and quickly strode through the crowded room and again took his place behind the table on the platform that had been set up yesterday. He slowly looked around at the assembled villagers. He knew that they had heard what he and Pring had done to Martha the night before and saw on some faces looks of fear, on others, expressions of respect for his power and on the faces of those that had been kin to the three victims there were looks of satisfaction.
The room fell silent and he nodded to John, the Meeting house warden who stood beside the door. It was opened and everyone turned around to see Martha's entrance.

If it had seemed that she was crippled and deformed before, to those who now saw her brought into the room it was as if a different woman had been summoned. Unable to stand or walk she was held up by Mark Pring and Richard Watten, the locksmith and gaoler.

There was now no trace of the calmness that had so shocked and surprised the villagers previously. The silence of the room was only broken by the scraping sound of Martha's shoes as she was dragged quietly groaning and almost semi-conscious towards where the witch finder sat behind the table waiting. He looked down at Martha. "Let a chair be brought" he ordered. There was a pause as one of the villagers brought a low stool which Martha was eased down upon with Pring still holding her by the arm.
John Norris's determined voice filled the room. "You are brought here again to answer the charges made of you yesterday. That you have by your witchcraft murdered or otherwise caused by your black arts, the deaths of three men of this village Edward Dent, Ralph Breton and Thomas Dekker. What do you now say to these charges?"
There was total silence as everyone waited for Martha's response but she made no answer, continuing to sit silently with her eyes now closed almost as if she were in another place far away. The Witchfinder spoke once more, his patience obviously coming to an end. " I ask you again, and I ask you for the last time. Do you make answer to these charges against you?"

A few moments of stilled silence followed which was suddenly broken and shattered by the terrifying screech of a raven as it flew in through the still open door and circled wildly around the room. There was a commotion with some women screaming and other people hurriedly crossing themselves. Memories came rushing back of that previous time at Ralph's burial and of what had been in the coffin with the body. Several men then stood up and made to catch the bird which continued to fly around before swooping low over Martha's head. Only now did she open her eyes and raise her head as the bird noisily flew across the room and out of the door.

As for Jared who up until a few moments before had been unable to tear his eyes away from the broken and beaten body of Martha and whose only effort had been to try and hide the deep satisfaction that filled his entire being at the sight. He too had looked up as the bird had flown through the door and then instinctively had brought his arms up to cover his face. He had heard the commotion and the screaming and above it all the terrifying cries of the bird and the sound of its beating wings.

"Silence" called out the strong voice of John Norris, and then again even louder," It was but a bird. We have business to do here. I call for silence."
The villagers responded and the room fell silent again though it was broken by the sound of a couple of women still sobbing in fear after the sudden interruption.
Only now did Jared feel able to lower his arms becoming aware that people were looking at him. He knew that he was shaking and that he must try to control himself. Anne was glaring at him and he tried to breathe deeply and calm down. A few moments passed and he felt better. There was even a sudden feeling of warmth, at first pleasing and then suddenly he flooded with shame as he realized that

like a child overcome by a nightmare, he had wet himself.

The Witchfinder looked down at Martha who had sat still and silent throughout the commotion. He looked around at the villagers. "Our Sovereign Majesty King James has himself said that witchcraft is treason against God and the only way to rid the world of such evils is to hunt down, arrest and execute the perpetrators, offering their life as a sacrifice to God."

Norris paused to let the full significance of the King's own words be understood. He returned his gaze back to Martha and continued. "You have brought evil into this village and done it harm. Above all else it is your very obstinate and unyielding silence which condemns you. That stubborn, willful silence that you showed here yesterday and indeed kept to even when put to the test. Your strength can only have come from that same Satan against whom we must all guard and fight. " He paused to let the full impact of his words carry around the meeting house.

"You shall be taken from here to Exeter where you shall stand trial for witchcraft at the next assizes. We shall leave at break of day tomorrow."

There was a murmur of assent from around the meeting house. Pring roughly brought Martha to her feet and with Watten's help, took her through the assembly and back to the lock-up. The villagers waited until John Norris had risen from his chair and also left before they silently dispersed, each to their own homes, each with their own thoughts.

Old Liza, the miller's wife was later to say that she had looked at Martha at the moment the bird had swooped above her and swore that Martha had smiled, but she was known to be addle brained and given to strange fancies and so was ignored.

That evening when they were all back in their homes the only talk was of the day's events. There were many who were disappointed that they would not see the ending of the drama that had come into their lives. There were others who only wished that the Witchfinder would have taken Martha away immediately and who would be uneasy and fearful until he did.
There were some who had been deeply shocked at the sight of the beaten and broken woman they had seen, although they fully understood the need for a witch to be put to the test. There were a few, very few, who had memories of Martha when she had lived among them those years before and only remembered a gentle if strange solitary girl. Among these were even some who felt pity and were sorry that, and indeed wondered why she had not spoken and saved herself from the suffering that had been inflicted on her.

In the home of Jared and Anne there was a silence that spoke of more than any words. For his part Jared felt nothing but pleasure and satisfaction at what had been done to Martha. The more so because he had feared that whatever threats he had made when he spoke with her would not hold her to silence if the pain were strong enough to break her will. He wanted nothing more than for her to be taken away and never to have sight or hear of her again.

No! That was not true he realized. He wanted to hear of her one last time, when the news would finally come from Exeter after the assizes and trial, that she was hanged and forever finished with. A sudden and disturbing thought came to him. Might Martha possibly speak out once she was away from the village? It was not a chance he could take. He resolved to speak with Norris in the morning and ask that he could accompany them back to Exeter.

For her part, Anne had been one of those shocked at what had been done to Martha. She had known her, lived with her, and despite the girl's many strange ways she had never thought her to be evil. Even the attack and injury she had suffered at Martha's hands those many years ago could be understood, after all, what would she have done in that situation? Anne had known her and indeed had also known Jared and she had no doubts about the man he was.

And finally, at the ending of that day, all in the village were in their beds and asleep, so there were none to witness as the snow silently and steadily began to fall.

49
Snow.

The next day the villagers woke to an unnatural brightness as the early morning April sunshine was reflected off a fall of snow that lay too deep even for some to open their doors. Snow in April. It was unusual but not unheard of. Normally such an event would be fun for the children and disruptive for the business of the village, but no more. This was different. Everyone knew that there would be no traveling to Exeter on this day. Nor as the day wore on and people were able to go outside and look at the sky, would there be the next day.

For the Witchfinder it was an inconvenience to be stuck in this village for even another day rather than be on his way back to Exeter with his captive.
For the villagers they were to be denied the spectacle of Martha being led away to her trial and what they all knew would be its inevitable conclusion.
For Jared it was something far more. Every day that Martha lived was another day in which she might finally speak. Speak and accuse. He knew that were she truly a witch or not, for him there would never be a moments rest or peace and indeed safety, until she was dead.
 He had trudged through the deep snow to the inn and asked permission from the Witchfinder to accompany them to Exeter to attend the trial. He had expressed the natural concern of a family member, and even though Norris had looked at him

with a strange and almost knowing expression, his request had been granted.

The day seemed to pass in a strangely slow way as if somehow time was suspended. People stayed within their homes, made a fire against the cold, talked about what it could all mean and wished for nothing more than to be able to get on with their everyday lives. Now and then they would get up and go and look out of their windows.
And still the snow fell.

That night the moon seemed to take on an eerie redness.
There were unnatural sounds that seemed to come winding through the narrow lanes of the village, causing dogs to bark, children to cry, and the villagers to become more fearful with every passing hour.
All said that when the sky cleared, the April sun would quickly melt the snow, but instead the temperature dropped and the snow hardened to ice, and on to that ice... more snow fell.

Old Goodwife Mary White who all those years before had brought Martha, as well as countless others of the village into the world had been ill and expected to die for a while, and so when she was found cold in her bed the next morning there were none who thought it strange. What had disturbed those who found her was the expression of terror on her lifeless face. It was also much spoken on that she had been heard to say that it were a bad night that she had helped at that birth and it would have been for the best had Elizabeth, the mother lived, and the baby died.

Not so with young Peter Wallis, the blacksmith's son, who it was said, had thrown a stone at Martha as she was being led by Mark Pring from the lock-up to the examination. He had gone out to play in the snow, had climbed a tree and fallen, breaking his neck.
And not so with farmer Mardell who had made his way through the deep snow to his milking shed where he had been crushed against a wall by one of his cows. It was remembered that he had been holding forth in his usual outspoken way that it was a waste of time taking Martha all the way to Exeter for a trial when it was obvious she was a witch and it were a pity that he would not be able to watch her hang right here in the village.
And more snow fell.

By the third day the village was in a state of panic. A deputation of the village elders and more important men went to Norris, who was still at the inn. What more signs of witchcraft did he need, they asked him. The weather itself had gone mad. Who knew when it would be possible to make the trip to Exeter. The village was cut off and it was obvious to all that there was a source of evil held within the lock up. Did he not have the King's own warrant to deal with it? Would he not act?

Norris, seated at a table with a jug of ale in front of

him and with Mark Pring by his side, glanced from one to another of the men. He thought for a few moments looking at the expectant faces He made his decision. Yes. He did have such an authority and indeed, he would use it.

And so, later that same afternoon, for the third time Martha was brought to the Meeting House, though this time there were far fewer villagers to witness this final act, most now convinced that whatever it was that had brought this nightmare to the village could be best dealt with by the King's Witchfinder.

Norris sat, as he had done twice before, as Martha was brought before him. This time there was no stool and she was supported between Pring and John Wallis, the father of young Peter who had broken his neck and lay cold and dead back in his cottage, with a grieving mother by his side.

There was no value to be gained by asking of Martha yet again if she would answer the charges. Norris wanted nothing more now than to speed the proceedings and return to the warmth of the inn. He paused for a few moments to let his words and the sentence he was about to pass make their full and dreadful effect. He placed his hand upon the Bible that sat on the table.

"By the authority of King James and also the words of our Holy Bible wherin it is written "Thou shalt not suffer a witch to live" I therefore do now pronounce upon you sentence of death. Tomorrow, here in the square of the village to which you have brought your evil you shall be hanged by the neck till you be dead and may that God against whom you have sinned show mercy to your soul."

He paused until the effect of the words of the sentence had brought total silence to those gathered in the meeting house room. He looked again at Martha whose head was slumped down. "Are there any words of confession or repentance that you now wish to make before these good people into whose midst you have brought your wicked and ungodly evils?"

There was a momentary murmur of conversation and then a hush fell across the room as people leaned forward ready to hear what Martha might now say. With an unbelievable slowness she lifted her head. She looked up to where Norris sat and opening her eyes looked directly into his.

John Norris had tried and sentenced many others before this woman. He had watched their tortures and executions and remained unmoved by their cries, their screams and their desperate pleas for mercy. In all that time he had never known pity or any other emotion other than the certain and unyielding belief that he was carrying out the will of both God and his own annointed sovereign, King James. This time there was something different. He looked away from Martha's gaze and let his eyes sweep the room and the faces of the few villagers who had attended. Though he did not want to, it seemed as if there was a strange power that compelled him to return his eyes to those of Martha. He drew a deep breath as he recognized the emotion that was now coursing through his entire body. It was fear! Aware of the villagers looking towards him he tried to calm himself. He brought his hands which had been resting upon the table tightly together so as to control the trembling that had begun in them. He grasped the Bible as if somehow it could take away this feeling that was overcoming him. He felt a dry tightness in his throat. Time seemed to be at a standstill. He took one gulped breath and closed his eyes, shutting out whatever it was that he had seen in Martha's, and called out in a voice that he realized was shaking. "Take the witch away."

..…..

In the cottage of Anne and Jared, the evening meal had been eaten in silence. After it was finished Anne sent Grace out to the barn to settle down the horse for the night and to check that all was in order. When she was gone, Anne said. "Tomorrow, I do not want Grace to go."
Jared looked at her in disbelief. "She be a child no longer. She must go. All of the village will be there, what would be said if we were absent. The Witchfinder himself expects everyone to attend. It is to see His Majesty's justice done."
Anne glared angrily at him as she replied, "And is it His Majesty's justice to see a woman put to death without any real proof being offered against her?"
"Are you mad woman" Jared answered. "Do you question the law? do you not know that the Witchfinder carries the King's warrant to do his business? She has brought her evil back into the village. Think of old Mary dying with that look on

her face, and then young Peter, and farmer Mardell. Even the weather that has come at this time of year. She has remained silent in spite of everything, she has surely condemned herself."

Anne was silent for a few moments and then looked directly into Jared's eyes. "She seemed willing enough to speak to you. So what was it she said when you met with her, you've not yet told me?" Anne paused "Or what was it that perhaps you said to her?"
Jared tried to think quickly. He had been stupid not to realize that Anne would have wanted to know. "I tried to ask her, tried to tell her, it would be better if she had owned to the murders "
Anne looked hard into Jared's face. "And tell me husband, if she had done them, what would have been the reason?"
"How is it that I should know, she was always strange, you had said so yourself many a time " he pointed to his scarred face "Look what violence she did to me when she was but a child, and also can you forget what she did to you on the night she ran from this house, did she not try to kill you."
Anne thought back to that dreadful evening all those years ago and how it had all come full circle. The anger had left her voice and she spoke quietly.
"I think now that it was for the sake of the baby. Had I let her take it with her, she would not have attacked me."
There was a long silence as Jared understood in a way he had not done before. "You mean you offered to let her go."

Ann slowly nodded. "There is a time for truth, and it is now. I did not feel towards her as you did. I wanted to save her. I wanted…" She stopped and looked away from Jared and into the fire "I wanted the baby. I cared not what happened to Martha. Better that she should have gone far away and made a new life, forgotten about all that had happened here"

"What do any of that matter now." he answered angrily "She will die tomorrow. It will all end as it should. The girl needs to be there to see. It will be a lesson to her."

A moments silence before Anne made her reply. "And what do you think it is that she will learn?" They both looked towards the door where Grace had just come back into the cottage.

"She will learn what comes of evil." said Jared as he turned sullenly away.

50
All save one.

Grace did not really know what it was that she was being taken to witness but as they came out of their house into the freezing cold day and began to trudge through the deep snow along the street towards the village square she became aware of some of the other villagers who were also going the same way glancing at her and whispering to each other.

They rounded the corner and came into the square where a crowd had already begun to assemble around a central space that had been cleared and where a tall post had been set up with a cross beam fixed to it, over which lay a rope at whose end was a noose. Leaning against the front of the post was a ladder. A bonfire in a metal brazier had been set up a few feet away against the biting cold where a few people were warming their hands. Jared and Anne with Grace between them took up a place at the edge of the square. There seemed to be a general feeling of excited anticipation mixed with a sort of restless nervous energy that Grace found hard to understand. She half knew from what she had overheard of the talk between Jared and Anne that this was to be some form of punishment for someone who had done something very bad.

The time seemed to be passing very slowly and with every moment Grace felt a growing yet inexplicable sense that whatever it was that she had been brought to see was somehow connected with

her and was going to change her forever.
A sudden silence came over all those gathered around the scaffold as the bell from the church tower rang out a solitary note and a small procession came into the square. It was led by John Norris, his black cloak held tight around him. Close behind him came the priest Henry Wilkin followed by Martha with her hands bound behind her back supported by Mark Pring and Richard Watten. She looked at none of the villagers but kept her eyes straight ahead towards the scaffold and the noose hanging down from the crossbeam.

Grace looked towards the procession as it made its way forwards and felt her entire body freeze and go into numbed shock as she looked beyond the bruised and bloodied face of the prisoner and suddenly recognized the condemned "witch" as none other than the woman who at Honiton market had given her the doll that now nestled within the folds of her apron.
 She turned towards Jared seeking an explanation of what was happening, but something in the expression on his face and the way he was watching the scene in front of him made her keep silent. She turned again to watch as the procession reached the centre of the square and the woman was helped, and half carried up the ladder that was leaning across the front of the post.
Between them, Mark Pring and Richard Watten eased Martha up the last few rungs. Pring moved up behind her and roughly positioned her at the top where he leaned across and taking hold of the

noose, pulled it over her head. He tightened the knot and climbed down the ladder.

The Witchfinder standing at the base of the scaffold moved forward a few steps and unfolding a piece of paper, began to read the sentence of death, his voice carrying across the square.
"Martha Carter. Having been found guilty of the charges of Witchcraft and of causing the deaths of three men of this village by unknown and evil practices you are to suffer death by hanging. If you have any final words to say before you are sent to God's own judgement, you may do so now."
There was total silence in the square as everyone waited out these last few moments, but Martha, her eyes closed in her bruised and battered face, remained silent.
Norris gave the order. "Let the punishment be carried out."

Grace looked around the square at the assembled villagers. At people she'd lived among and had known all her life and saw that they were all somehow changed by this spectacle they had come to witness. There was Richard Watten, now having moved away from the ladder, arms folded and watching with an expression of grim satisfaction on his face. There was James the innkeeper, looking on as if the scene were no more than a maypole dance. There was old mistress Catherine Brown with what could only be described as a strangely cruel smile on her face. Over there was young Ellen Parry and her husband standing together, she with her two-week-old baby in her arms. There were Robert and Peter the builder's apprentices grateful for the free time they had been allowed away from work. And of course there were the families of the murdered men, each in their own way hoping that what they were about to witness might perhaps ease their pain and anger and with their faces set hard in anticipation of seeing justice done. She looked around at them all and realized that what was missing were any expressions of compassion or sympathy.

Grace looked back towards the centre of the square where Mark Pring had now taken hold of the ladder and was now waiting for the sign from Norris. The Witchfinder quickly glanced towards the woman now balanced on the top of the ladder as if somehow seeking to reassure himself that the feelings he had experienced the day before in the Meeting house when he had passed sentence were just a momentary and irrational fear.
Thankfully her eyes were closed. He felt an uncontrollable shudder begin to run through him as he suddenly knew with certainty that through those closed eyes...She was looking at him.
He nodded to Pring who tightened his grip on the ladder and quickly pulled it away.

There was a collective gasp from the gathered crowd as Martha swung down with the noose tightening around her throat and beginning to squeeze the life out of her. Her legs began to kick wildly, and her broken body twisted with agony.

Her blackened eyes opened and began to bulge, and the strangled sounds of her choking filled the entire square.

Grace felt she was going to be sick. She tried to look away from the dreadful scene, but Jared forced her head back towards the awful spectacle which seemed never ending.

Sometimes at a hanging there would be friends or members of the condemned's family who would rush forward and pull at the legs to try and shorten the agony. But there were none who would do this for Martha and as her body still moved in its grotesque death dance, Grace looked around the square and could see no signs of pity for what was taking place. She finally looked at Jared and realized that not only was there no vestige of pity but rather a cruel smile on his face.

Finally, after what seemed the longest time, it was over. Martha's body hung lifelessly at the end of the noose. Her head lay at an unnatural twisted sideways angle to her body where the rope's knot had been fixed. Her mouth hung open and her dead eyes were fixed in an empty stare. There was utter silence among the assembled villagers who stood as if transfixed looking at the body as it slowly swung to and fro.

Still silently, one or two villagers slowly turned away and began to leave the square. Others began to follow also without any words being spoken. It was as if a line had been drawn that marked the end of the nightmare that had started weeks ago with

Edward's murder. Of course they would all remember the events for ever. The deaths and the horrors, the trial and the hanging. But now it would be time to move on. They all had their own lives to live.

Suddenly there was a piercing scream as Catherine Brown pointed at Martha's body.
which had begun to move.
Everyone in the square turned their eyes towards the horrifying spectacle as Martha, still swinging at the rope's end began to speak, her voice forcing through bloodied and swollen lips and rising up over all those who had gathered to watch her death. And they were not the words that anyone had expected to hear. They were not cries for forgiveness and salvation, or prayers to a merciful God. They were words of pure hate.

" I lay the curse of a wronged woman upon you all."

Tremors of fear and shock ran through everyone there, with people shouting and screaming and so not hearing her clearly as she repeated her dreadful words.
 "I lay the curse of a wronged woman upon you all...
All save one."

And though Grace felt she would have given anything to be able to look away she now realized that even if it was against her will, there was something stronger forcing her to look again

towards the hanged woman, who in turn was looking across the square and all the other people, directly and only at her.
And she was smiling.

And now, only now, did Jared break out of what had seemed a trance at what was happening and rush forward towards the scaffold where he wildly grabbed at her legs and began to pull down on the body with all his strength.

His heart was pounding as if it would burst. The shock and fear that was overwhelming him seemed to be taking his very strength so that as hard as he was pulling, he could feel the body above him still moving.

Finally he seemed to be winning the battle and he felt any resistance leave the legs he was grasping. He fought against his fear and looked upwards into Martha's face. He had been wrong. It was not over. Her blood red eyes stared down into his for one last time as her dying words came.

"We will wait for you."

51
Fire.

It was over.
Though there was nothing left to see, the villagers remained where they were, unsure of themselves, whether to stay and see if there were to be any final words of direction from the Witchfinder or to leave and return to their homes. A few of them had made the sign of the cross. Some of the men had slowly removed their hats and there was the crying of a few of the children who had either been forced or who had even wanted to witness the scene.

Up until now, from the time of Martha's capture all had been expectation leading up to what they had just witnessed. Now somehow, strangely there seemed to be a common yet unspoken sense of unease among the crowd. No-one was sure of what to do, not wanting to be seen as to first to turn away from the scene of the King's justice and leave, lest the eye of the Witchfinder might take that as sympathy with the condemned.

There was a general feeling that Norris was about to speak. To make some comment on what had happened, when there suddenly came with a strange almost sighing sound a soft breeze blowing and winding through the streets that led to the market square whipping up little flurries of the still deep snow as it came.
People nervously looked to the Witchfinder, for surely, he had seen many other hangings and would know what to do. Instead, he stood among them

with as much bewilderment and unease on his face as anyone else, watching with all the others as Jared remained at the foot of the scaffold clinging onto the hanged woman's legs.

There seemed to be a mysterious kind of spell holding everyone fixed to wherever they stood, wanting to flee and at the same time unwilling, or unable to move, with the unspoken fear among them that Martha's dying curse might have taken hold.

"The King's justice has been done. Go now back to your homes."

The commanding voice of Norris rang out across the square at which people immediately snapped out of their trance like attitudes and began to turn away in grateful response to the Witchfinder's bidding.

What had only a few moments ago seemed like a whispering breeze now strengthened into a wind that blew more of the fallen snow into the air and around the square.

Then suddenly one great and final gust of wind caught at the bonfire which now seemed to glow for a few moments brighter than the noonday sun before exploding and sending red hot burning shards and ashes showering over the crowd. Now what had been silence was broken by shouting and screams as the burning embers fell against flesh and onto clothes which immediately caught fire. There was panic as everyone began to run in different directions, colliding with each other to escape from the square.

In his hurry to flee Richard Watten pushed old Catherine Brown out of the way. She fell backwards against the base of the bonfire where her dress burst into flame. In moments she was engulfed by fire, with her agonized screams only adding to the fear of terrified villagers. On the other side of the square Ellen Parry in her rush for safety, tripped over a piece of burning wood which had fallen from the bonfire and fell to the ground dropping her small baby which within seconds had been trampled under the feet of a dozen people. At the edge of the square Robert the builder's lad was cradling Peter's head in his arms. A splinter of burning wood had entered his eye and blinded him.

Jared had released his grip on Martha's body and had turned away from it with a wild and terrified expression on his ashen face. He ran back to where Anne and Grace stood and grabbing at them both, started to fight his way through the crowd pushing people out of the way so as to escape the madness. They left the panic of the square and rushed into the lane which led back to their cottage. It seemed a miracle, but they had somehow escaped unharmed from the nightmare scene. Whatever Martha's power had been it was finished now, and he was free and unharmed. His heart was pounding as he led the way towards the safety of home. Anne had not spoken a word and on Grace's face there was the same look of shock that had been there since she had first seen Martha dragged out for her hanging.

They could still hear the screams coming from the

square although these were now becoming fainter as they ran on. Jared looked up and saw in the sky above him swirls of smoke carrying glittering embers away from the deadly scene they had just left. They turned down the final bend that led to their home. They stopped and stood transfixed, speechless and horror struck as they looked towards the end of the lane where angry flames were taking hold of the thatched roof of the barn next to the cottage.

Jared ran forward. He couldn't believe what was happening. The few brief moments of relief he had experienced once he knew Martha could no longer hurt him now vanished. He reached the barn and frantically rushed inside to bring out the horse. Anne and Grace had now caught up with him and he handed the bridle to Anne as he turned and went back inside the barn for the cart.
By now several villagers had come to help and some went in the barn to carry out any equipment that could be saved whilst others tried to pull at the thatch to prevent the flames spreading.
Though his body was responding to the urgent task of stopping the flames from taking hold, it was as if his mind was working independently.
It seemed to Jared as if the horror of the day were never ending. He had woken that morning with the belief that by the end of the day it would all be finished. Martha would be dead, taking with her any knowledge of what had happened in the past. He would finally be safe. He would finally be free.

Eventually after a couple of hours they were successful, and the fire was stopped. The villagers who had helped returned to their own homes. Jared, his face smoke blackened, and his clothes dirtied and torn walked inside the cottage, poured himself a jug of ale and slumped down into a chair. Anne and Grace followed without a word.

In the cottage that evening there was a stunned silence as Jared, Anne and Grace tried to make sense of and come to terms with what had happened in just a few short hours.

For her part Grace was still overcome by the horror of what she had been forced to witness. Beyond that horror though lay so many questions, but she knew with certainty that there was no one who could...or would, answer them. She felt only relief when Anne told her to go to her bed where the only comfort she found was as she held Hope close.

Her mind went back to when it had been given to her in the market by the woman who in her thoughts and memory she would now always see hanging and twisting at the end of a rope as life was slowly and agonizingly choked out of her.

Apart from the hanging and what had come after... the explosion, the panic and the fire, there was so much that she could not even begin to understand. How had a hanged woman come suddenly to life again? How was it possible for her to have smiled despite the agony, and to have cursed the entire village?

She remembered the woman's final words. She had

said... "*All save one.*"
Grace didn't understand the connections between the woman, the crimes for which she was being hanged and what she had said. What she did know beyond doubting was that she was the one that had been meant.

As she lay in her bed with so many thoughts and images crowding her mind, she felt the comforting warmth that seemed to come from the doll she held beneath the thin rough blanket that covered her. The doll that had been gifted to her by the woman. The doll that had been ripped apart, buried, and then had miraculously been made whole again. The doll she had held beneath her apron in the village square and that had somehow given her the will to watch the awful spectacle

She brought the doll closer to her face and whispered her thoughts and her questions. Among all of them was one that spun around and around in her mind. "Who was she...who was she?"

And Hope told her.

…..

Once Grace had gone to bed and Anne felt she would be asleep and unable to hear them she looked across to where Jared still sat silent and motionless.
"What did she say to you?"
Jared looked at Anne with a guarded expression on his face.
"Don't pretend you don't know" she said angrily. "At the end when you pulled at her legs. She spoke to you. I saw it...everyone did."

"It...it were nothing. I couldn't hear. I couldn't understand what she were tryin' to say."

"Then why did you look as if you'd been struck with a hammer as you let go and turned away?"

"It were the shock of it all." Jared replied weakly. "And then we come back and the barn be on fire."

Anne thought for a moment before answering. "And why do you think that it were our barn?"

Jared's face changed. There was now a sly look as he spoke. "It do prove that she were a witch. I knew it from the day she were born...even at the end she was tryin' to do her evil. You heard her curse the whole village just like the time she done in the church."

"All save one " Anne said softly.

Jared made no answer. He didn't want to speak. He didn't want to think, and above all...he did not want to remember the last words that had come from Martha's strangled throat.

52
Leaving

The next day, though the snow was still deep, John Norris and Mark Pring left Clanton at first light, hoping that once they were away from the village and over the surrounding hills the going might be easier. They were prepared to accept a long and difficult journey back to Exeter rather than have to stay and await better weather. The village itself seemed quiet and deserted. Some villagers peeped out from behind their windows but for the most part the feeling was that it was better to forget all that had happened... the horror of Martha's hanging, and especially what came after.

A little way outside the village they were surprised to see a young girl standing by the side of the track. They pulled their horses to a halt and the Witchfinder looked down at her.
 She was looking up at him somehow questioningly, almost as if she had been there waiting to ask something of him. She was obviously one of the village children and he had known this to happen before, where one of the younger ones would want to ask a question about what they had witnessed, though in truth it had only ever been one or a couple of the village boys and in his remembering, never a girl. The whole matter was over and done with and he felt that he could spare the few moments it would take to humour her.
"What do you do out here child?" Norris asked.
There was no answer in return. Mark Pring

addressed her in a harsher tone.

"Did you not hear what you were asked? Have you not been taught to answer when your elders and betters speak to you?"

Again there was no response. Mark began to dismount. "What this child needs is to be taught a lesson."

"Leave her" Norris said. "We have not the time for this, the girl is probably simple minded like most of the others in that accursed place." He spurred his horse and began to move away followed by Pring. who a few yards on, turned in his saddle and then gave a short laugh. " You were right, she do be simple minded." Norris also then turned around and saw the young girl just standing in the snowy track looking after them and talking to a small doll she held.

As the morning passed, the sun came up and though weak was still enough to thaw some of the snow-covered countryside they rode through. By mid-day they had crossed the hills that surrounded the village and were able to make better speed and began to look forward to returning to Exeter and their homes. For his part John Norris was still uneasy that he had exceeded his authority in not bringing the accused witch back with them to stand trial. Now that they had left the village far behind them, he seemed able to think more clearly. What choice had been open to him he reasoned. The village was surely in the grip of something evil, even the weather had conspired to hold them all captive for who knows how long. People were dying, it was his duty to take action, it was only what would have been expected of him.

They decided to halt for a brief while to eat the bread, meat and cheese they had been given by James, the keeper of the inn where they had been staying, and to finish off the flask of ale he had sent them away with.
Having finished they remounted their horses and continued along the track.
After another hour had passed John Norris began to feel unwell. There was a pain in his stomach and a feeling of bile in his mouth. He turned to Pring. "I have a pain in my gut which may be from that food we ate or perhaps it was the ale, it had a taste of bitterness about it.".
Pring looked across at him and laughed "It tasted good to me. Perhaps you but need to stop and clear yourself out."
Norris allowed himself a weak smile. "Perhaps you are right, we'll stop here."
They reined in their horses and Norris passed his bridle to Pring and dismounted. He walked a few paces to the side of the track, set aside his heavy cloak and pulled down his breeches. After a few minutes of straining and heaving he was done and remounted his horse with a satisfied sigh of relief.
Pring looked at him "All well?" The Witchfinder nodded his head "All well."

By the early evening they had made good time as they had hoped. Strangely the snow seemed less with every mile they rode closer to Exeter almost as if its falling and settling in such depth had been centred on the village. Also with every mile Norris felt more able to set aside any doubts he'd had about his decision to hang the witch. He had the King's authority to help cleanse the realm of all such infestations and he was confident that he could answer any questions about what had happened back there in that remote and unimportant village. Swift and decisive action had been called for and that is what he had delivered.

There was something else though, at the outer edges of his mind. It was somehow unsettling though he could not understand why. He had taken part in many other witch questionings; he had seen other hangings. What was there about this one that was so different, apart from the admittedly strange phenomenon of a supposedly dead corpse speaking. Obviously, the witch had not been fully dead and had found some secret inner strength, or indeed witchcraft, to be able to make her final cursing words sound out across the village square. He thought about the way that other than her screams of pain, she had said not a single word through all of what he and Pring had done to her. He remembered the way she had looked at him at the questioning with an expression that spoke more than words. He remembered the way it had made him feel.

All finished and done with. They would return to Exeter and he would make his report to the justices. He would doubtless even be commended for the way he had dealt with the whole business.

Finally they crested a hill and pulling their horses to a halt by the side of some trees, looked towards the city of Exeter in the distance. In the slowly darkening light they could make out wispy trails of smoke rising from the chimneys and Norris thought of the people who would be huddling around their home fires or perhaps enjoying a mug of ale and good company in one of the many taverns.

Rising above all the city he looked towards the two towers of the Cathedral Church of St Peter that dominated the skyline. Norris made a promise to himself that after a good night's sleep, he would go on the morrow and give thanks for his safe return from what had been a troubling journey. He would light a candle in the peace of the Lady Chapel and feel the comfort that would come from the sure knowledge that he had done God's own work.
"Almost there" said Mark Pring. "We will make it by nightfall." He looked to John Norris who was also gazing towards the city but was also clutching at his stomach. "Has the gut pain returned?" he asked. "Perhaps you need another emptying."
The Witchfinder nodded. "I feel it in more than my gut which feels like it is burning, but everywhere else there is a coldness in me."
"I have coldness too but is it not just the weather?" answered Pring, his voice betraying impatience at the thought of another stop, even whilst the end of their journey was finally in sight "Another hour or so and we'll be in the city and we will find warmth there. Let us travel on now."
John Norris shook his head. "I must but rest for a

while till the feeling passes. Help me down."
Mark Pring wearily dismounted and moved to the side of Norris's horse. He helped the Witchfinder to the ground.
"Let me lay against there for a moment." said Norris looking towards the nearest of the trees.
"Help me with my cloak and spread it down."
Pring unfastened the heavy black cloak and laid it on the ground. He took Norris by the arm and eased him down against the trunk.
"I want to face the city." said Norris still holding his stomach, his face now sweating and creased with pain.
"Do you want me to do anything?" asked Pring suddenly becoming fearful as he looked into Norris's face which he could see, even in the gloom was taking on a white pallor? "Do you wish me to..."
The voice of the Witchfinder was weak but firm. "I wish you not to speak. Just stand away and by the horses. I wish only to be alone and to look towards the city."
Mark Pring did as he was told and moved away a few feet, standing by the side of the horses.

Laying against the tree, Norris felt momentarily rested. The pain in his stomach seemed to have passed, though the other feeling of a coldness still held and indeed seemed to be spreading throughout his body. There came a different and contrasting sense of warmth underneath him. With a sudden sense of shame he realized that the reason the pain in his stomach had gone was that he had had fouled himself. He wanted nothing more than to be able to stand up, remount his horse and finish the journey, to throw away his ruined clothes, clean himself and to be able to sleep.

He knew that none of these things would happen. He turned his eyes away from the city, from the homes and taverns, and even from the Cathedral. He looked to the now rapidly darkening sky. It was empty, save for a lone bird that wheeled high above, now flying down closer almost as if to look at him before turning away towards the city he now knew he would never again enter.

He realized he was dying though he could not understand why or how. Could there truly have been something in that curse the witch had uttered even after she was thought to be dead. He closed his eyes and remembered what she had looked like, and then suddenly became aware of what had been unsettling him ever since they had left the village. He had seen the face of the witch again, and it was on that of the young girl who had been standing... or was it waiting, for them that morning. With what felt to be a huge and final effort he opened his eyes again, but there was nothing to see.

Or was there everything?

53
Questions.

And in the village, the snow had melted. April had turned to May, but for the first time in anyone's memory there seemed to be no enthusiasm or will to hold a May fair and as if with an unspoken assent none was held.
The terrible events of the day of the execution had changed the village forever. Those who had died in the explosion of the bonfire and the panic that had followed had been laid to rest in the churchyard. Martha's body had been taken from the village and buried in an unmarked grave close to an old oak tree near the riverbank.

The witch had been caught, brought to justice and executed. The scaffold had been taken down. The Witchfinder and his assistant had left the village. The fear had ended and somehow life had returned to its natural order and yet…and yet.
There was somehow a feeling of emptiness in the village, of something unfinished. Questions remained, things that were spoken of only in the privacy of people's homes. Why would Martha have returned after so many years to take a revenge on the men who had died and what had they been to her? Why would she not have spoken or answered any of the questions put to her by the Witchfinder and how could she have remained silent through all the pain? What could have brought the strange weather that had trapped them in their own village and prevented the witch being taken away, allowing

her evil to kill even more people? And what of that final horror at her hanging.

Questions…so many questions, and nowhere were they thought of more than in the home of Jared and Anne. Thought of, though not spoken. Since the evening of the hanging when Anne had asked Jared what Martha had said to him there was a look that had come into Anne's face that Jared had found more searching and unsettling than anything she could have asked.

 Beyond it all though, as the days and then the months passed Jared felt more and more at ease. Unbelievable though it had seemed, Martha had endured the torture and not spoken. Their secret had died at the end of a noose. The only other witnesses to what had really happened those years ago on the cliff and what had been done to Matthew were also dead. Martha had been caught and hanged before she had had a chance to kill him as she must surely have intended. It would all pass he thought, and life would go on as ever before. He was surely safe. That was what he told himself every day.
 But the nights were different. When he closed his eyes and when he wished for nothing more than to fall into a deep and comforting sleep, he remembered only those final words. The words that thanks be to God no-one else had heard. When he did sleep, he heard them in his dreams, and when he woke, they were the start to his day.

"We will wait for you."

54
Wanting.
May. 1625

The years changed. The seasons turned. On a blustery and rain swept day in March, King James died. His son Henry who had been Prince of Wales and heir to the throne had died thirteen years earlier, and so James was succeeded by his second son Charles. Another new age was surely dawning. The twenty-two-year reign had brought many changes. There was now a union between England and James's original homeland of Scotland. The religion of the country seemed to be settled, with the plot to blow up the King and his Parliament twenty years before now a distant memory, though some had felt disquiet at the new King Charles's choice of bride when he had married the Catholic Henrietta Maria of Spain.

The years of the late King's reign had been mainly peaceful and surely among all the changes and achievements of those years was that the kingdom had for the most part been cleansed of the foul curse of witchcraft.

And nowhere was that cleansing felt more than in Clanton. Over four years had passed with no more signs of witchcraft or any other manifestations of evil.

Those who had died, and the manner of their deaths were surely remembered, but life had to go on. There was work to be done, and as ever had been, that work was hard and continuous. People sometimes spoke of the dead but tried only to talk of their lives rather than of what had come at the ending of those lives. Of the witch and her hanging there was, as if by common agreement, no public mention ever made.

In their own homes however, there would always be talk and speculation regarding everything surrounding those past events. Jared and Anne continued with their lives which were increasingly unhappy. The sharpness of Anne's tongue and temper meant that there were few other villagers who wanted to spend any more time with her than was needed to greet her when passing.
 As for Jared, though he himself had escaped any evil that his witch of a sister might have done to him, it was as if he carried the curse that Martha had spoken almost like a contagion. He continued to work as a carter and would mix with the others of the village only insofar as any mutual business made it necessary. When he carried the goods and produce of other villagers to market or delivery, at the end of the day's work he would be paid and thanked. Nothing more, no conversations or going to the inn together for some well-earned tankards of ale and company.

And it was in that inn one evening in May that he sat as he always did, on his own in the corner and reflected as now he seemed to do increasingly often on what had been his life. He had had but the three friends, Edward, Ralph and Thomas and they were gone, murdered by that bitch Martha. He wondered where had his life gone so wrong. He raised his hand and touched the side of his face, the rough skin coming to seem more puckered and deformed with every passing year. Yes, it was all from that time the witch... for now he truly understood that was what she surely had been, had attacked him. He thought for a few moments. No! It was long before that. It was when he was a child and had sat in the corner of the cottage for endless hours through that night, when his whole world was filled by the sound of his dying mother's screaming.

He thought of his years with Anne. It had never really been good, but since Martha's return, capture and then that awful day of the hanging and then the fire, it had grown steadily worse. She repulsed him. She had grown fat, and the sourness that had always been in her nature was now deeply etched in her face. He took a swallow of his ale and silently cursed. Was this all there was ever going to be? Was there never again to be anything other, anyone other? and finally, as he downed more of the ale that suddenly somehow seemed as bitter as his life, he thought of Grace.

Jared knew then what he had hardly dared admit to himself. In the years of her growing he had feared that she might resemble him, that others in the village would see, would guess and come to believe what Martha had shouted out in the church. They would know for certain who her real father was. But now instead, she was coming to be daily more like her mother.

As she was surely leaving the years of childhood behind and turning into a young woman she was beginning to look like Martha, to sound like her, even to walk the way she had done. Jared could see all of this and he knew that just as he had felt about her mother... he hated her.

And he knew that he wanted her.

At night as he lay next to Anne in the coldness of their bed, he imagined how it would feel to have Grace's young body next to him. To be able to take her as he had taken Martha, to see again that same look on her face. She would struggle, she would fight, but in the end, he would overcome her...he would possess her.
He turned the image over and over in his mind. He knew where he would do it. He knew the place she held as secret and how she often would go there whenever her work was done. He smiled to himself at the memory of what else had happened in that place. Yes, it would be fitting that it should be there. It was her secret place.

But also his.

55
Trapped

Three days later the chance came. Anne had gone to visit with Catherine, Edward's widow who had moved a few miles away. He had watched as Grace having finished her housework had quietly walked out from the cottage as she often did at this time of day before she needed to start preparing their evening meal. He saw he go towards the path that led over the old bridge and away from the village. He waited a few moments and then set out to follow her. He knew where she would go. He knew where he would find her.

As he made his way out of the village and on to the path that would take him into the woods and towards the river, his thoughts went back to that time years before when he and the others had settled with Matthew. He suddenly realized that it had been at this same time of the year when spring was moving towards summer.
Even now, all these years later he felt a pleasing satisfaction as he remembered the events of that day and the helplessness of the young man held between Edward and Ralph as he had punished him for what had happened that day in the market.
He remembered the sight of Matthew in the river fighting for breath as he'd realized there was no escape possible. He also thought of the others, Edward, Ralph and Thomas. So strange that he alone was left now. He tried to push the thoughts of what had happened to them out of his mind. He

smiled. He did not need their assistance for what he was soon going to do.

Jared came along the path and with a mounting sense of anticipation walked to the edge of the clearing. He paused behind a tree to watch her for a moment, feeling the wanting and excitement move through his body. He saw her sitting at the base of the large oak. She was holding a doll and seemed to be talking to it. He stepped out and moved towards her.
Instead of the fear and shock he had expected to see on her face she looked at him calmly. No matter, he thought. Her almost insolent calmness would soon be over. This was surely the time and the place.
"It's time to be done with dolls now" he said harshly "Dolls are for children not for women."
She looked at him questioningly, "And am I a woman uncle? I am but sixteen years"
In spite of the unease Jared felt at the way she had spoken he forced a mocking laugh. "You will be a woman once I have done with you."

He came to her side and reaching down to grab her arm he roughly pulled Grace to her feet. With his right arm he held her against the tree and with his free hand he began to lift her dress. Strangely she did not struggle but instead seemed ready to accept what was going to happen. For a moment he thought it almost a pity as he knew he would have enjoyed it more if she had fought against it as Martha had done. Her body was relaxed, almost yielding. He released his grip on her and began to pull at his breeches. He looked into her face, trying to understand the expression in her eyes, and then just beyond her face at the bark of the tree. For a moment he was puzzled by what looked like two initials carved into the tree which seemed at first glance to be entwined within a heart design.

All of a sudden Grace's body seemed to come alive and he felt a savage stinging as she clawed at his face. For a moment the change in her behavior made him suddenly think back to when Martha had scalded and then scarred him all those years ago. He put his hand to his face, feeling the blood her nails had drawn. "You bitch " he shouted "You're just like your mother, I did for her and I'll finish you…I'll…"

The look that had come over Grace's face cut through his anger as she spoke now in a voice that somehow did not even seem to be her own. "And what did you do for her Uncle? or should I say what did you do to her... Father?"

Jared felt his blood run cold at the words and the sound of her voice. She knew! How did she know. Had she guessed or had someone told her, and if so...Who?

He made to grab at Grace again, but she had twisted free from the hand that held her and began to run further down the track. For a couple of moments he was too shocked by what she had done...and said, to move. Suddenly the possibility of her escaping forced him into action. He started to chase after her as she ran through the shelter of the trees. For a few moments he lost sight of her and could feel the panic starting to clutch at him. She knew! She knew, and even if he caught her, even if he beat or threatened her, what might she say to Anne? He understood then what he would have to do, and with that realization he also knew where the track led, and that there would be no escape for her.

He came through the trees and looked towards where Grace stood with her back to him, motionless by the riverbank, silently staring across at the other side. This was it! She was trapped. She would surely know that. He felt a sudden calming determination coming to him. It was almost over. He would have her... and then he would kill her. He made another sudden decision. That would then be an end to it. He would be free of them all, the village, Martha, Anne, the girl...all of the past. He would go away and start again.
He moved towards where she remained motionless and without any chance of escape. Another few steps and he reached her, and as he did, she slowly turned around to face him. He stopped as if rooted to the earth. Instead of the terrified fear he was expecting to see on her face there was only…

A strange smile.

56
The River

For a moment, the world and all the time it contained seemed to stand still. It was a warm and sunny day and yet he felt the air grow cold all around him and what was even worse...within him.
"Look at me."
He saw her lips move and knew she was speaking, but with a voice he had never heard before.
Suddenly there was no more lust in him and no more anger. There was only fear. He willed himself to move, to turn away, to run, but it was impossible. He closed his eyes.
"Look at me."
He knew there was nothing he could do but obey. He slowly opened his eyes. Grace had moved closer to him and as she stared up into his face it was as if her eyes grew larger with hidden depths into which he was falling.
And as he looked into them, he saw.
He saw Edward, with that dying look of terror on his face as his throat was being sliced open. He saw Ralph, screaming as he fell headlong from the tower and towards the ground rushing to claim him. He saw Thomas, wild eyed stricken and dying in absolute horror after drinking the ale.
Yes...and he also saw Martha reeling backwards from his punch and falling over the cliffs.

Grace moved to one side and slowly raising her arm pointed towards the river. He felt movement come back into his limbs, but it was not a movement that he could control. He could not do other than allow himself to walk the few steps down the bank and towards the river. He came to the edge and as if in a dream or rather a nightmare, stepped into the ice-cold water. He waded a few more paces in, then turned and looked imploringly towards Grace. He knew she could help him…save him…stop this madness. All he had to do was to beg her forgiveness. He opened his mouth to call out to her, but no words came. Instead what did come to him was the sound of Grace singing softly to the doll which she was still holding. He tried to understand the meaning of the words that he heard. Were they meant for him or the doll?

"We waited long and yet we knew, This day would come, for me...for you.
A life will end here. A life of sins. One story closes...and one begins"

She stopped singing and he saw with horror that both her arms were outstretched and that she was holding the doll towards where he stood with the running water now rising as his feet, as if acting without his will, moved him further out into the deeper part of the river.
 It was madness but somehow above his uncomprehending fear the thought came to him that it was as if she wanted the doll to see him….to witness this moment.

Helplessly he felt the water now reaching his waist. He willed his eyes to close and shut out the sight of

Grace and the doll standing there on the riverbank watching him, but strangely it was as if unseen fingers were refusing to let him and were instead forcing them wide open again.

He was overwhelmed by a torrent of emotions. There was anger and fear. There was rage and regret. His mind was spinning, and the journey of his entire life seemed to be of no other purpose than that he should be here…now…at this moment and at this place. He suddenly remembered that it was exactly where he had sat by the riverside as a grief stricken eight-year-old boy after the death of his mother. Other thoughts and memories came rushing back and with a shock he realized that he was standing in the same part of the river where all those years before they had finished with Matthew.

And then…

It was as if the riverbed beneath his feet was shifting and becoming less firm…like sand…like mud.

He felt himself stumbling and being drawn down under the water. He was gasping for breath and trying somehow to resist but the current seemed to pull at him with an incredible strength. He tried to move his arms and swim away but was powerless, caught between Grace's unremitting fixed stare from the river bank and the strong force taking him under. He wondered for a moment whether his feet might be entangled in some river weed that he could free himself from, and then suddenly and with a fear that clutched at and then squeezed his heart he realized that whatever held him by his feet was

tightening its grip. It was madness…it felt like...
Fingers!

Long fingers grasping and clawing and pulling him under. In that moment his mind seemed to clear, and it was as if he knew. He understood that this was where and how it was going to end. He looked once more to where Grace stood impassively by the riverbank still with the doll held out towards him and he realized with a deep and heartbreaking sadness that this was the last image he would ever see on this earth and in this life.
He was wrong !

As his head went below the water and the remaining few bubbles of his life's breath left his fear stricken and paralysed body, there was one final horrifying sight. And he knew what…he knew who, had been grasping at his legs and pulling him down to a watery grave.
And he understood Martha's final words.

"We will wait for you."

57
A New Dawn.

May 1625.

She had spent the night in the woods but without any fear. It was almost as if there would never be any fear again. The night time sounds had all seemed to have a message for her. The call of the owl, the whispering of the wind through the branches of the trees, the scurrying of creatures through the undergrowth. She felt at one with everything around her. She was part of the natural world and it was also within her.
It was all as it had been meant to be. It had not been hard for her to wait out the time. She had known that she could not have left any earlier and had always believed that this day would come. She had kept the power that she knew she possessed to herself, guarding and cherishing it. She knew she would not be followed, and was now able to make her own way.

At first light in the early morning she had woken and looked to the doll that had lain next to her through the night. It had been her friend and companion since that day years before when it had been given to her by the woman she now knew to have been her mother. She lovingly caressed it, stroking its now long hair and feeling the warmth it held from its closeness to her own body throughout the night. It had ever been a constant in her life since the day she had first received it.

It was the same as it had been on that day, and on the day it had been torn apart by the village children. It was the same as it had been when she had raised it out of the grave she had dug for it. It was the same as it had been at the riverside as Jared was pulled beneath the water. Except...
The serious, somewhat sad expression on its face was gone.
...and it was smiling.

Grace rose to her feet and gently bedded it down into her pocket. She looked towards the rising sun and knowing it to be in the east she began to walk towards the west. And on that May dawn, anyone watching a young girl walking down the lonely track, away from the village, the riverbank, and all that had gone before and towards the distant and waiting city of Exeter, would have witnessed a scene that was almost identical to one that had taken place sixteen years before.
 Then there had been falling snow and icy cold. But now, despite the early hour, there was some warmth in the air and the promise of a fine new day. Also this time there were no pursuers, and the girl would reach her destination. Wherever that was to be.
And if they had perhaps for a moment looked away from the girl and upwards into the pale dawn streaked sky, they might also have seen circling... or perhaps following.

A raven.